③ attainment. He

for something that _____ ... ... _____ ever been

done or that others have tried and

failed. Then sometimes, with great

luck, he will succeed.

¶ How simple the writing of

literature would be if it were only

necessary to write in another way

what has been well written. It

is because we have had such great

writers in the past that a writer is

driven out far out past where

he can go, far out to where no

one can help him.

¶ I have spoken too long for a writer. A writer

S thank you and Again

Ernest Hemingway.

how to say and not speak it ⓧ

should write what he

ALSO BY ERNEST HEMINGWAY

Ernest Hemingway

THE OLD MAN AND THE SEA

THE HEMINGWAY LIBRARY EDITION

Foreword by PATRICK HEMINGWAY

Edited with an introduction by SEÁN HEMINGWAY

SCRIBNER

New York   London   Toronto   Sydney   New Delhi

Scribner
An Imprint of Simon & Schuster, Inc.
1230 Avenue of the Americas
New York, NY 10020

This Scribner hardcover edition July 2020

SCRIBNER and design are registered trademarks of The Gale Group, Inc., used under license by Simon & Schuster, Inc., the publisher of this work.

For information about special discounts for bulk purchases, please contact Simon & Schuster Special Sales at 1-866-506-1949 or business@simonandschuster.com.

The Simon & Schuster Speakers Bureau can bring authors to your live event. For more information or to book an event, contact the Simon & Schuster Speakers Bureau at 1-866-248-3049 or visit our website at www.simonspeakers.com.

Manufactured in the United States of America

9   10

Library of Congress Cataloging-in-Publication Data has been applied for.

ISBN 978-1-4767-8784-8
ISBN 978-1-4767-8786-2 (ebook)

To Charlie Scribner

and

Max Perkins

Contents

Foreword

In his treatise *On the Nature of Things*, the ancient Roman philosopher Lucretius once wrote: "Life is one long struggle in the dark." What I think he meant by that is there is so much that we do not know. My own education began in many ways during the summers of my youth in Key West, Bimini, and Cuba, especially at Finca Vigía, with my father, who was a wonderful teacher. Cuba and the Gulf Stream then were like an Eden for me, and returning to boarding school always felt like being sent into exile from paradise. Fishing trips with Papa aboard the *Pilar* in pursuit of marlin, exploring the sea by snorkeling with some of the first single-lens goggle glasses, and the trove of natural history books in my father's library awakened me to the world in all of its beauty and complexity. In *The Old Man and the Sea*, Santiago knows about life's struggle—he has fished for eighty-four days without a catch. He is not, however, entirely in the dark. In my view, a great achievement of this novel is how my father, drawing on his own formidable experience and talent, managed to create for us the world of the Gulf Stream so completely. It is a powerful evocation of a precious ecosystem, one sadly undergoing terrible changes today due to human intervention, and one very much worth protecting.

In a fascinating twist of history, the Austrian physicist Erwin Schrödinger and Ernest Hemingway died in the same year. Over the course of their lives both men made great contributions to their chosen professions, each achieving a Nobel Prize, one in physics, the other in literature. Perhaps the most memorable of the Austrian physicist's thought experiments was "Schrödinger's cat"—a creature both dead and alive at the same time. It was a way for him to explain the duality of conditions that can coexist in quantum physics. Schrödinger imagined a cat in a closed box with a deadly poison—one would not know if the cat was dead or alive and so it would, in a sense, be both. Part of the mythic power of *The Old Man and the Sea* is something that I would call "Hemingway's cat." A seemingly impossible feat is made possible through my father's storytelling: an old man alone in a skiff on the sea manages to bring in a fish weighing over a thousand pounds.

Patrick Hemingway

Introduction

The Old Man and the Sea is arguably the greatest fishing story of all time. It ranks, in my opinion, above Herman Melville's *Moby-Dick* as the most marvelous piscatorial contribution of American literature. It is a timeless story—mythic, archetypal—but it is also of its time. Like the whaling industry of nineteenth-century America captured so poignantly in *Moby-Dick*, the practice of Cuban commercial fishermen setting out in small sailing skiffs for large billfish, using only hand tackle, is now largely a thing of the past with the advent of motorboats and modern fishing equipment.[1]

Fishing has been a part of human experience for thousands of years and this story reminds us of its importance.[2] Part of the joy of reading *The Old Man and the Sea* is the portrayal of the act of fishing itself, as anyone who has held a hand line or a rod with a fish tugging on it will understand. Fishing, for those of us who practice it, is one of life's great pleasures. I am forever grateful to my father for introducing me at a young age to the wonders of fishing, as his father had done for him. The notion of passing on this knowledge from generation to generation, which is expressed so beautifully in the novella through the friendship of Santiago and the young boy, is an important aspect of the story.

How did Ernest Hemingway come to write this master-piece? *The Old Man and the Sea* had a long period of gestation. In 1936 Hemingway described the essence of the story in an article he wrote for *Esquire* magazine entitled "On the Blue Water: A Gulf Stream Letter," included as the first appendix to this book. It was a tale told to him by Carlos Gutiérrez, a Cuban fisherman who taught my grandfather much about big-game fishing (see figs. 1–3). Hemingway's passion for deep-sea fishing began much earlier, though, and it was through his determination to master the sport that he acquired a wealth of detailed knowledge enabling him to write the novella many years later.

Hemingway first became interested in deep-sea fishing when he lived in Key West in the late 1920s, which is also when he began to visit Cuba. The personal fishing logs he kept for more than ten years are preserved in the Ernest Hemingway Collection at the John F. Kennedy Presidential Library and Museum in Boston. They document everything from the numerous fishing trips and catches he made to the weather conditions.[3] In a log from 1932 there are notes from conversations with Carlos Gutiérrez that record fascinating tips about fishing for marlin, as well as the fish's behavior and characteristics (see fig. 2). In the spring of 1934, upon returning from the safari that he immortalized in *Green Hills of Africa*, Hemingway custom-ordered his own deep-sea fishing boat. The *Pilar*, a forty-two-foot wooden motor cruiser from the Wheeler Shipyard in Brooklyn, was to become his home on the sea (see figs. 3–5). By the following year my grandfather had caught more than one hundred marlin (see fig. 6) and was considered enough of an expert to write authoritative articles about the sport.[4] He was approached by scientists from the Academy of Natural Sciences of Philadelphia and the American Museum of Natural History in New York to help gather information about the large game fish of the Gulf Stream—their classifications, life histories, diets, migratory patterns, and mating habits.[5] The ichthyologist Henry Fowler even recognized his contributions by naming a new species of sculpin after him, *Neomerinthe hemingwayi*.[6] One of the largest marlin that Ernest Hemingway ever fought, which was arguably nine hundred pounds, was hooked by his friend Henry Strater on the *Pilar* in 1935. As Hemingway describes in a letter just after the event (appendix II), the fish was savagely attacked by sharks while they reeled it in and lost nearly half of its meat. It is clear that my grandfather drew on this real-life experience when he wrote *The Old Man and the Sea*.

Hemingway had a great number of encounters with sharks and caught several large makos, one of which, hooked near Bimini, was 786 pounds. This Hemingway Library Edition includes as appendix III a previously unpublished list by my grandfather of principal sharks in Cuban waters (see fig. 10). It features his own observations about the different species and how dangerous they become when they smell blood in the water. Hemingway even pioneered a technique for quickly landing large fish to avoid their being attacked by sharks. In the summer of 1935 in Bimini, he was the first angler to bring in a bluefin tuna unscathed by sharks.

A particularly exciting feature of this Hemingway Library Edition of *The Old Man and the Sea* is the inclusion of a previously unpublished short story by my grandfather (see appendix IV, fig. 11), which Patrick Hemingway has aptly entitled "Pursuit As Happiness." The story makes a marvelous counterpart to *The Old Man and the Sea* and gives a vivid sense of what it was like for Hemingway when he went deep-sea fishing for marlin in those early days. Set in 1933, the story describes Hemingway's passionate pursuit of a huge marlin while aboard the *Anita*, a ship captained by my grandfather's friend Josie Russell, who owned both the *Anita* (see fig. 1) and Sloppy Joe's Bar in Key West. The story uses nonfictional characters like my grandfather and his longtime first mate Carlos Gutiérrez (see figs. 1 and 3). It is difficult to say how much of it is based on fact and how much was embellished by the storyteller. Certain elements, such as the reference to outriggers, which were added to the *Pilar* in April 1935, indicate that the story was written much later than 1933.[7] Will Watson in his careful study of my grandfather's fishing logs notes how he became disappointed with the aging Gutiérrez in 1936, as his first mate made more and more mistakes on the *Pilar* resulting in many lost fish. These later experiences may have inspired Hemingway's fictional account of Carlos's error in the short story.[8] Other details suggest the autobiographical nature of the story. The main character resides at the Ambos Mundos Hotel, where Hemingway first stayed in Havana, and eats and drinks at the Floridita, which was one of his favorite hangouts. He also mentions his own record of catching seven white marlin in one day off the north coast of Cuba, a record Hemingway held alone until 1936.[9] The heroic notion of giving all of the meat away to the locals is a happy and generous way to ensure that none of the meat from their fishing adventures went to waste. However, what happens in the story contrasts with the reality in Bimini during the 1930s, when massive quantities of trophy fish meat went unused.

It was a common occurrence that deeply bothered my grandfather.[10]

Hemingway periodically returned to the idea of writing *The Old Man and the Sea*. In a letter to his editor Max Perkins in 1939, he mentions that it would make a great addition to a forthcoming book of short stories:

> . . . And three very long ones I want to write now. One about Teruel called Fatigue. One about the old commercial fisherman who fought the swordfish all alone in his skiff for 4 days and four nights and the sharks finally eating it after he had it alongside and could not get it into the boat. That's a wonderful story of the Cuban coast. I'm going out with old Carlos in his skiff so as to get it all right. Everything he does and everything he thinks in all that long fight with the boat out of sight of all the other boats all alone on the sea. It's a great story if I can get it right. One that would make the book.[11]

No other record of that trip with Carlos Gutiérrez exists, but Hemingway's personal collection of photographs, many taken by the author himself, show Cuban fishermen at work in their small wooden sailing boats with typically two men aboard (see figs. 7 and 8). A photo of a Cuban fishing boat with a large marlin nearly the length of the skiff gives a powerful sense of the heroic nature of these fishermen and their quarry (see fig. 9).[12]

The onsets of the Spanish Civil War (1936–1939) and World War II (1939–1945) led my grandfather to other writing projects, and it was not until the end of 1950 that he was finally able to write the story of the old fisherman.

At that time he had completed the first draft of a novel that would be posthumously published as *Islands in the Stream*.[13] Hemingway had envisioned this manuscript as the first book of a major trilogy that he was composing on "The Sea, The Air and The Land."[14] As Hemingway wrote *The Old Man and the Sea*, he thought it could serve as a coda to the sea book.[15] By February 17, 1951, he had completed the first draft (26,531 words) of *The Old Man and the Sea* at Finca Vigía. Preferring to rise early in the morning and work until lunchtime, he claimed to have written 1,000 words per day for a sixteen-day period that month, much more than his usual output.[16]

During this time the young, beautiful Adriana Ivancich, who was the model for the female heroine in *Across the River and Into the Trees*, was visiting the Finca with her mother, and she once again provided inspiration for my grandfather's writing.[17] Hemingway even suggested that Adriana illustrate the story. Her artwork, drawn from visits to the little fishing village of Cojímar, was used for the cover of the book (see fig. 15). In a moment of generosity before the book was even published, Hemingway gave the original manuscript to Adriana's brother Gianfranco Ivancich.[18] Unfortunately, that manuscript has never been found. Hemingway's final typescript with quite a number of pencil corrections in the author's hand is preserved in the Ernest Hemingway Collection at the John F. Kennedy Presidential Library and Museum. It illustrates some of the last editorial changes that Hemingway made to *The Old Man and the Sea*. For the most part, these changes are minor additions that clarify or reinforce his existing statements. For example, in the first paragraph of page 1, he adds the words "now definitely and finally" before "*salao*, which is the worst form of unlucky," and he makes clear that it was the boy's parents who sent him to work on a boat other than Santiago's (see fig. 12). On page 96 of the typescript he adds an evocative description of how the shark sinks into the sea (fig. 13). Some forty-four emendations are included in appendix V, which represent nearly all of the changes that were made by the author at this late stage. The final text as it was published varies very little from this typescript.[19]

After sharing the completed manuscript with his wife, Mary; Charles Scribner; and several friends, including the movie producer Leland Hayward, Hemingway decided that it would be best published as a novella. The story, at the time of its publication, also appeared as a single issue of *Life* magazine on September 1, 1952 (see fig. 14). In a comment to the editors of *Life*, Hemingway wrote that he was excited so many people who could not afford to buy the book would be able to read the story in the magazine. Such accessibility, he wrote, made him happier than if he had received the Nobel Prize, a rather brash, faux denial of his interest in this greatest of accolades.[20] The novella was immensely successful from the moment of its publication. The five-million-copy run in *Life* sold out within two days and the book itself, published by Charles Scribner's Sons, went straight to the *New York Times* bestseller list, where it remained for twenty-six weeks. Among the many glowing reviews, William Faulkner wrote: "His best. Time may show it to be the best single piece of any of us, I mean his and my contemporaries."[21]

During this time, my grandfather wrote to the noted art historian Bernard Berenson: "Then there is the other secret. There isn't any symbolism. The sea is the sea. The old man is the old man. The boy is the boy and the fish is the fish. The sharks are all sharks, no better and no worse."[22] In truth and as generations of scholars have shown, *The Old Man and the Sea* certainly has more symbolism than most of Hemingway's stories.[23] There is much that lies beneath the surface of the deceptively simple language: like the dignity of an iceberg, seven-eighths of its mass lies beneath the water, as my grandfather was fond of saying.[24]

In 1953 Hemingway received the Pulitzer Prize for *The Old Man and the Sea*, and the following year he was awarded the Nobel Prize in Literature, the citation of which mentions *The Old Man and the Sea* as an important work. This Hemingway Library Edition includes my grandfather's Nobel Prize acceptance speech (appendix VI). In an early draft, Hemingway joked about the source of Nobel's money—dynamite—and in a later draft he soberly wrote: "There is no lonelier man than the writer when he is writing except the suicide. Nor is there any happier, nor more exhausted man when he has written well."[25] The final acceptance speech, pared down to its essence, poignantly echoes the narrative of the novella: "It is because we have had such great writers in the past that a writer is driven far out past where he can go, out to where no one can help him." *The Old Man and the Sea* was the last major work of fiction that my grandfather would complete in his lifetime, and it remains among his very best.

During the summer of 2019, I went hiking with my family to a remote cave on the eastern shore of Crete. We harvested salt from crevices in the rocks along the coast and swam in the cool, clear water of the Aegean Sea. While snorkeling amid schools of colorful fish on the edge of a shelf that dropped more than a hundred feet, I came face-to-face with two small tuna that appeared out of the great blue abyss. I thought about *The Old Man and the Sea* as I walked back across the barren, rugged landscape. The sun was high and the wind was blowing hard from the south. I made my own path along the bright red earth between sharp wind-etched, low-lying stones and patches of purple flowering thyme, their gnarled roots clinging to the surface. Suddenly a Cretan wild hare bounded from a nearby bush, startling me. I stopped and watched him tear off for about sixty yards before disappearing into the landscape. Moments later as I continued on my way, a covey of partridges shot out with the wind, their fluttering wings making a great whirring noise next to me. I thought again of *The Old Man and the Sea* and how Santiago is able to read the sea, which to the untrained eye looks vast and undifferentiated. He understands all its signs—from the shape of the clouds in the sky to the significance of birds chasing schools of small fish. Hemingway's prose and its clear descriptive details bring the Gulf Stream to life. When you read the story you too will come to understand a remarkable ecosystem as it existed not long ago, and you will see it through the eyes of a fisherman with a profound respect for the sea.

Seán Hemingway

THE OLD MAN
AND THE SEA

He was an old man who fished alone in a skiff in the Gulf Stream and he had gone eighty-four days now without taking a fish. In the first forty days a boy had been with him. But after forty days without a fish the boy's parents had told him that the old man was now definitely and finally *salao*, which is the worst form of unlucky, and the boy had gone at their orders in another boat which caught three good fish the first week. It made the boy sad to see the old man come in each day with his skiff empty and he always went down to help him carry either the coiled lines or the gaff and harpoon and the sail that was furled around the mast. The sail was patched with flour sacks and, furled, it looked like the flag of permanent defeat.

The old man was thin and gaunt with deep wrinkles in the back of his neck. The brown blotches of the benevolent skin cancer the sun brings from its reflection on the tropic sea were on his cheeks. The blotches ran well down the sides of his face and his hands had the deep-creased scars from handling heavy fish on the cords. But none of these scars were fresh. They were as old as erosions in a fishless desert.

Everything about him was old except his eyes and they were the same color as the sea and were cheerful and undefeated.

"Santiago," the boy said to him as they climbed the bank from where the skiff was hauled up. "I could go with you again. We've made some money."

The old man had taught the boy to fish and the boy loved him.

"No," the old man said. "You're with a lucky boat. Stay with them."

"But remember how you went eighty-seven days without fish and then we caught big ones every day for three weeks."

"I remember," the old man said. "I know you did not leave me because you doubted."

"It was papa made me leave. I am a boy and I must obey him."

"I know," the old man said. "It is quite normal."

"He hasn't much faith."

"No," the old man said. "But we have. Haven't we?"

"Yes," the boy said. "Can I offer you a beer on the Terrace and then we'll take the stuff home."

"Why not?" the old man said. "Between fishermen."

They sat on the Terrace and many of the fishermen made fun of the old man and he was not angry. Others, of the older fishermen, looked at him and were sad. But they did not show it and they spoke politely about the current and the depths they had drifted their lines at and the steady good weather and of what they had seen. The successful fishermen of that day were already in and had butchered their marlin out and carried them laid full length across two planks, with two men staggering at the end of each plank, to the fish house where they waited for the ice truck to carry them to the market in Havana. Those who had caught sharks had taken them to the shark factory on the other side of the cove where they were hoisted on a block and tackle, their livers removed, their fins cut off and their hides skinned out and their flesh cut into strips for salting.

When the wind was in the east a smell came across the harbour from the shark factory; but today there was only the faint edge of the odour because the wind had backed into the north and then dropped off and it was pleasant and sunny on the Terrace.

"Santiago," the boy said.

"Yes," the old man said. He was holding his glass and thinking of many years ago.

"Can I go out to get sardines for you for tomorrow?"

"No. Go and play baseball. I can still row and Rogelio will throw the net."

"I would like to go. If I cannot fish with you, I would like to serve in some way."

"You bought me a beer," the old man said. "You are already a man."

"How old was I when you first took me in a boat?"

"Five and you nearly were killed when I brought the fish in too green and he nearly tore the boat to pieces. Can you remember?"

"I can remember the tail slapping and banging and the thwart breaking and the noise of the clubbing. I can remember you throwing me into the bow where the wet coiled lines were and feeling the whole boat shiver and the noise of you clubbing him like chopping a tree down and the sweet blood smell all over me."

"Can you really remember that or did I just tell it to you?"

"I remember everything from when we first went together."

The old man looked at him with his sun-burned, confident loving eyes.

"If you were my boy I'd take you out and gamble," he said. "But you are your father's and your mother's and you are in a lucky boat."

"May I get the sardines? I know where I can get four baits too."

"I have mine left from today. I put them in salt in the box."

"Let me get four fresh ones."

"One," the old man said. His hope and his confidence had never gone. But now they were freshening as when the breeze rises.

"Two," the boy said.

"Two," the old man agreed. "You didn't steal them?"

"I would," the boy said. "But I bought these."

"Thank you," the old man said. He was too simple to wonder when he had attained humility. But he knew he had attained it and he knew it was not disgraceful and it carried no loss of true pride.

"Tomorrow is going to be a good day with this current," he said.

"Where are you going?" the boy asked.

"Far out to come in when the wind shifts. I want to be out before it is light."

"I'll try to get him to work far out," the boy said. "Then if you hook something truly big we can come to your aid."

"He does not like to work too far out."

"No," the boy said. "But I will see something that he cannot see such as a bird working and get him to come out after dolphin."

"Are his eyes that bad?"

"He is almost blind."

"It is strange," the old man said. "He never went turtle-ing. That is what kills the eyes."

"But you went turtle-ing for years off the Mosquito Coast and your eyes are good."

"I am a strange old man."

"But are you strong enough now for a truly big fish?"

"I think so. And there are many tricks."

"Let us take the stuff home," the boy said. "So I can get the cast net and go after the sardines."

They picked up the gear from the boat. The old man carried the mast on his shoulder and the boy carried the wooden box with the coiled, hard-braided brown lines, the gaff and the harpoon with its shaft. The box with the baits was under the stern of the skiff along with the club that was used to subdue the big fish when they were brought alongside. No one would steal from the old man but it was better to take the sail and the heavy lines home as the dew was bad for them and, though he was quite sure no local people would steal from him, the old man thought that a gaff and a harpoon were needless temptations to leave in a boat.

They walked up the road together to the old man's shack and went in through its open door. The old man leaned the mast with its wrapped sail against the wall and the boy put the box and the other gear beside it. The mast was nearly as long as the one room of the shack. The shack was made of the tough budshields of the royal palm which are called *guano* and in it there was a bed, a table, one chair, and a place on the dirt floor to cook with charcoal. On the brown walls of the flattened, overlapping leaves of the sturdy fibered *guano* there was a picture in color of the

Sacred Heart of Jesus and another of the Virgin of Cobre. These were relics of his wife. Once there had been a tinted photograph of his wife on the wall but he had taken it down because it made him too lonely to see it and it was on the shelf in the corner under his clean shirt.

"What do you have to eat?" the boy asked.

"A pot of yellow rice with fish. Do you want some?"

"No. I will eat at home. Do you want me to make the fire?"

"No. I will make it later on. Or I may eat the rice cold."

"May I take the cast net?"

"Of course."

There was no cast net and the boy remembered when they had sold it. But they went through this fiction every day. There was no pot of yellow rice and fish and the boy knew this too.

"Eighty-five is a lucky number," the old man said. "How would you like to see me bring one in that dressed out over a thousand pounds?"

"I'll get the cast net and go for sardines. Will you sit in the sun in the doorway?"

"Yes. I have yesterday's paper and I will read the baseball."

The boy did not know whether yesterday's paper was a fiction too. But the old man brought it out from under the bed.

"Perico gave it to me at the *bodega*," he explained.

"I'll be back when I have the sardines. I'll keep yours and mine together on ice and we can share them in the morning. When I come back you can tell me about the baseball."

"The Yankees cannot lose."

"But I fear the Indians of Cleveland."

"Have faith in the Yankees my son. Think of the great DiMaggio."

"I fear both the Tigers of Detroit and the Indians of Cleveland."

"Be careful or you will fear even the Reds of Cincinnati and the White Sox of Chicago."

"You study it and tell me when I come back."

"Do you think we should buy a terminal of the lottery with an eighty-five? Tomorrow is the eighty-fifth day."

"We can do that," the boy said. "But what about the eighty-seven of your great record?"

"It could not happen twice. Do you think you can find an eighty-five?"

"I can order one."

"One sheet. That's two dollars and a half. Who can we borrow that from?"

"That's easy. I can always borrow two dollars and a half."

"I think perhaps I can too. But I try not to borrow. First you borrow. Then you beg."

"Keep warm old man," the boy said. "Remember we are in September."

"The month when the great fish come," the old man said. "Anyone can be a fisherman in May."

"I go now for the sardines," the boy said.

When the boy came back the old man was asleep in the chair and the sun was down. The boy took the old army blanket off the bed and spread it over the back of the chair and over the old man's shoulders. They were strange shoulders, still powerful although very old, and the neck was still strong too and the creases did not show so much when the old man was asleep and his head fallen forward. His shirt had been patched so many times that it was like the sail and the patches were faded to many different shades by the sun. The old man's head was very old though and with his eyes closed there was no life in his face. The newspaper lay across his knees and the weight of his arm held it there in the evening breeze. He was barefooted.

The boy left him there and when he came back the old man was still asleep.

"Wake up old man," the boy said and put his hand on one of the old man's knees.

The old man opened his eyes and for a moment he was coming back from a long way away. Then he smiled.

"What have you got?" he asked.

"Supper," said the boy. "We're going to have supper."

"I'm not very hungry."

"Come on and eat. You can't fish and not eat."

"I have," the old man said getting up and taking the newspaper and folding it. Then he started to fold the blanket.

"Keep the blanket around you," the boy said. "You'll not fish without eating while I'm alive."

"Then live a long time and take care of yourself," the old man said. "What are we eating?"

"Black beans and rice, fried bananas, and some stew."

The boy had brought them in a two-decker metal container from the Terrace. The two sets of knives and forks and spoons were in his pocket with a paper napkin wrapped around each set.

"Who gave this to you?"

"Martin. The owner."

"I must thank him."

"I thanked him already," the boy said. "You don't need to thank him."

"I'll give him the belly meat of a big fish," the old man said. "Has he done this for us more than once?"

"I think so."

"I must give him something more than the belly meat then. He is very thoughtful for us."

"He sent two beers."

"I like the beer in cans best."

"I know. But this is in bottles, Hatuey beer, and I take back the bottles."

"That's very kind of you," the old man said. "Should we eat?"

"I've been asking you to," the boy told him gently. "I have not wished to open the container until you were ready."

"I'm ready now," the old man said. "I only needed time to wash."

Where did you wash? the boy thought. The village water supply was two streets down the road. I must have water here for him, the boy thought, and soap and a good towel. Why am I so thoughtless? I must get him another shirt and a jacket for the winter and some sort of shoes and another blanket.

"Your stew is excellent," the old man said.

"Tell me about the baseball," the boy asked him.

"In the American League it is the Yankees as I said," the old man said happily.

"They lost today," the boy told him.

"That means nothing. The great DiMaggio is himself again."

"They have other men on the team."

"Naturally. But he makes the difference. In the other league, between Brooklyn and Philadelphia I must take Brooklyn. But then I think of Dick Sisler and those great drives in the old park."

"There was nothing ever like them. He hits the longest ball I have ever seen."

"Do you remember when he used to come to the Terrace? I wanted to take him fishing but I was too timid to ask him. Then I asked you to ask him and you were too timid."

"I know. It was a great mistake. He might have gone with us. Then we would have that for all of our lives."

"I would like to take the great DiMaggio fishing," the old man said. "They say his father was a fisherman. Maybe he was as poor as we are and would understand."

"The great Sisler's father was never poor and he, the father, was playing in the Big Leagues when he was my age."

"When I was your age I was before the mast on a square rigged ship that ran to Africa and I have seen lions on the beaches in the evening."

"I know. You told me."

"Should we talk about Africa or about baseball?"

"Baseball I think," the boy said. "Tell me about the great John J. McGraw." He said *Jota* for J.

"He used to come to the Terrace sometimes too in the older days. But he was rough and harsh-spoken and difficult when he was drinking. His mind was on horses as well as baseball. At least he carried lists of horses at all times in his pocket and frequently spoke the names of horses on the telephone."

"He was a great manager," the boy said. "My father thinks he was the greatest."

"Because he came here the most times," the old man said. "If Durocher had continued to come here each year your father would think him the greatest manager."

"Who is the greatest manager, really, Luque or Mike Gonzalez?"

"I think they are equal."

"And the best fisherman is you."

"No. I know others better."

"*Qué va*," the boy said. "There are many good fishermen and some great ones. But there is only you."

"Thank you. You make me happy. I hope no fish will come along so great that he will prove us wrong."

"There is no such fish if you are still strong as you say."

"I may not be as strong as I think," the old man said. "But I know many tricks and I have resolution."

"You ought to go to bed now so that you will be fresh in the morning. I will take the things back to the Terrace."

"Good night then. I will wake you in the morning."

"You're my alarm clock," the boy said.

"Age is my alarm clock," the old man said. "Why do old men wake so early? Is it to have one longer day?"

"I don't know," the boy said. "All I know is that young boys sleep late and hard."

"I can remember it," the old man said. "I'll waken you in time."

"I do not like for him to waken me. It is as though I were inferior."

"I know."

"Sleep well old man."

The boy went out. They had eaten with no light on the table and the old man took off his trousers and went to bed in the dark. He rolled his trousers up to make a pillow, putting the newspaper inside them. He rolled himself in the blanket and slept on the other old newspapers that covered the springs of the bed.

He was asleep in a short time and he dreamed of Africa when he was a boy and the long golden beaches and the white beaches, so white they hurt your eyes, and the high capes and the great brown mountains. He lived along that coast now every night and in his dreams he heard the surf roar and saw the native boats come riding through it. He smelled the tar and oakum of the deck as he slept and he smelled the smell of Africa that the land breeze brought at morning.

Usually when he smelled the land breeze he woke up and dressed to go and wake the boy. But tonight the smell of the land breeze came very early and he knew it was too early in his dream and went on dreaming to see the white peaks of the Islands rising from the sea and then he dreamed of the different harbours and roadsteads of the Canary Islands.

He no longer dreamed of storms, nor of women, nor of great occurrences, nor of great fish, nor fights, nor contests of strength, nor of his wife. He only dreamed of places now and of the lions on the beach. They played like young cats in the dusk and he loved them as he loved the boy. He never dreamed about the boy. He simply woke, looked out the open door at the moon and unrolled his trousers and put them on. He urinated outside the shack and then went up the road to wake the boy. He was shivering with the morning cold. But he knew he would shiver himself warm and that soon he would be rowing.

The door of the house where the boy lived was unlocked and he opened it and walked in quietly with his bare feet.

The boy was asleep on a cot in the first room and the old man could see him clearly with the light that came in from the dying moon. He took hold of one foot gently and held it until the boy woke and turned and looked at him. The old man nodded and the boy took his trousers from the chair by the bed and, sitting on the bed, pulled them on.

The old man went out the door and the boy came after him. He was sleepy and the old man put his arm across his shoulders and said, "I am sorry."

"*Qué va*," the boy said. "It is what a man must do."

They walked down the road to the old man's shack and all along the road, in the dark, barefoot men were moving, carrying the masts of their boats.

When they reached the old man's shack the boy took the rolls of line in the basket and the harpoon and gaff and the old man carried the mast with the furled sail on his shoulder.

"Do you want coffee?" the boy asked.

"We'll put the gear in the boat and then get some."

They had coffee from condensed milk cans at an early morning place that served fishermen.

"How did you sleep old man?" the boy asked. He was waking up now although it was still hard for him to leave his sleep.

"Very well, Manolin," the old man said. "I feel confident today."

"So do I," the boy said. "Now I must get your sardines and mine and your fresh baits. He brings our gear himself. He never wants anyone to carry anything."

"We're different," the old man said. "I let you carry things when you were five years old."

"I know it," the boy said. "I'll be right back. Have another coffee. We have credit here."

He walked off, barefooted on the coral rocks, to the ice house where the baits were stored.

The old man drank his coffee slowly. It was all he would have all day and he knew that he should take it. For a long time now eating had bored him and he never carried a lunch. He had a bottle of water in the bow of the skiff and that was all he needed for the day.

The boy was back now with the sardines and the two baits wrapped in a newspaper and they went down the trail to the skiff, feeling the pebbled sand under their feet, and lifted the skiff and slid her into the water.

"Good luck old man."

"Good luck," the old man said. He fitted the rope lashings of the oars onto the thole pins and, leaning forward against the thrust of the blades in the water, he began to row out of the harbour in the dark. There were other boats from the other beaches going out to sea and the old man heard the dip and push of their oars even though he could not see them now the moon was below the hills.

Sometimes someone would speak in a boat. But most of the boats were silent except for the dip of the oars. They spread apart after they were out of the mouth of the harbour and each one headed for the part of the ocean where he hoped to find fish. The old man knew he was going far out and he left the smell of the land behind and rowed out into the clean early morning smell of the ocean. He saw the phosphorescence of the Gulf weed in the water as he rowed over the part of the ocean that the fishermen called the great well because there was a sudden deep of seven hundred fathoms where all sorts of fish congregated because of the swirl the current made against the steep walls of the floor of the ocean. Here there were concentrations of shrimp and bait fish and sometimes schools of squid in the deepest holes and these rose close to the surface at night where all the wandering fish fed on them.

In the dark the old man could feel the morning coming and as he rowed he heard the trembling sound as flying fish left the water and the hissing that their stiff set wings made as they soared away in the darkness. He was very fond of flying fish as they were his principal friends on the ocean. He was sorry for the birds, especially the small delicate dark terns that were always flying and looking and almost never finding, and he thought, the birds have a harder life than we do except for the robber birds and the heavy strong ones. Why did they make birds so delicate and fine as those sea swallows when the ocean can be so cruel? She is kind and very beautiful. But she can be so cruel and it comes so suddenly and such birds that fly, dipping and hunting, with their small sad voices are made too delicately for the sea.

He always thought of the sea as *la mar* which is what people call her in Spanish when they love her. Sometimes those who love her say bad things of her but they are always said as though she were a woman. Some of the younger fishermen, those who used buoys as floats for their lines and had motorboats, bought when the shark livers had brought much money, spoke of her as *el mar* which is masculine. They spoke of her as a contestant or a place or even an enemy. But the old man always thought of her as feminine and as something that gave or withheld great favours, and if she did wild or wicked things it was because she could not help them. The moon affects her as it does a woman, he thought.

He was rowing steadily and it was no effort for him

since he kept well within his speed and the surface of the ocean was flat except for the occasional swirls of the current. He was letting the current do a third of the work and as it started to be light he saw he was already further out than he had hoped to be at this hour.

I worked the deep wells for a week and did nothing, he thought. Today I'll work out where the schools of bonito and albacore are and maybe there will be a big one with them.

Before it was really light he had his baits out and was drifting with the current. One bait was down forty fathoms. The second was at seventy-five and the third and fourth were down in the blue water at one hundred and one hundred and twenty-five fathoms. Each bait hung head down with the shank of the hook inside the bait fish, tied and sewed solid and all the projecting part of the hook, the curve and the point, was covered with fresh sardines. Each sardine was hooked through both eyes so that they made a half-garland on the projecting steel. There was no part of the hook that a great fish could feel which was not sweet smelling and good tasting.

The boy had given him two fresh small tunas, or albacores, which hung on the two deepest lines like plummets and, on the others, he had a big blue runner and a yellow jack that had been used before; but they were in good condition still and had the excellent sardines to give them scent and attractiveness. Each line, as thick around as a big pencil, was looped onto a green-sapped stick so that any pull or touch on the bait would make the stick dip and each line had two forty-fathom coils which could be made fast to the other spare coils so that, if it were necessary, a fish could take out over three hundred fathoms of line.

Now the man watched the dip of the three sticks over the side of the skiff and rowed gently to keep the lines straight up and down and at their proper depths. It was quite light and any moment now the sun would rise.

The sun rose thinly from the sea and the old man could see the other boats, low on the water and well in toward the shore, spread out across the current. Then the sun was brighter and the glare came on the water and then, as it rose clear, the flat sea sent it back at his eyes so that it hurt sharply and he rowed without looking into it. He looked down into the water and watched the lines that went straight down into the dark of the water. He kept them straighter than anyone did, so that at each level in the darkness of the stream there would be a bait waiting exactly where he wished it to be for any fish that swam there. Others let them drift with the current and sometimes they were at sixty fathoms when the fishermen thought they were at a hundred.

But, he thought, I keep them with precision. Only I have no luck anymore. But who knows? Maybe today. Every day is a new day. It is better to be lucky. But I would rather be exact. Then when luck comes you are ready.

The sun was two hours higher now and it did not hurt his eyes so much to look into the east. There were only three boats in sight now and they showed very low and far inshore.

All my life the early sun has hurt my eyes, he thought. Yet they are still good. In the evening I can look straight into it without getting the blackness. It has more force in the evening too. But in the morning it is painful.

Just then he saw a man-of-war bird with his long black wings circling in the sky ahead of him. He made a quick drop, slanting down on his back-swept wings, and then circled again.

"He's got something," the old man said aloud. "He's not just looking."

He rowed slowly and steadily toward where the bird was circling. He did not hurry and he kept his lines straight up and down. But he crowded the current a little so that he was still fishing correctly though faster than he would have fished if he was not trying to use the bird.

The bird went higher in the air and circled again, his wings motionless. Then he dove suddenly and the old man saw flying fish spurt out of the water and sail desperately over the surface.

"Dolphin," the old man said aloud. "Big dolphin."

He shipped his oars and brought a small line from under the bow. It had a wire leader and a medium-sized hook and he baited it with one of the sardines. He let it go over the side and then made it fast to a ring bolt in the stern. Then he baited another line and left it coiled in the shade of the bow. He went back to rowing and to watching the long-winged black bird who was working, now, low over the water.

As he watched the bird dipped again slanting his wings for the dive and then swinging them wildly and ineffectually as he followed the flying fish. The old man could see the slight bulge in the water that the big dolphin raised as they followed the escaping fish. The dolphin were cutting through the water below the flight of the fish and would be in the water, driving at speed, when the fish dropped. It is a big school of dolphin, he thought. They are widespread and the flying fish have little chance. The bird has no chance. The flying fish are too big for him and they go too fast.

He watched the flying fish burst out again and again and the ineffectual movements of the bird. That school has gotten away from me, he thought. They are moving out too fast and too far. But perhaps I will pick up a stray and perhaps my big fish is around them. My big fish must be somewhere.

The clouds over the land now rose like mountains and the coast was only a long green line with the gray blue hills behind it. The water was a dark blue now, so dark that it was almost purple. As he looked down into it he saw the red sifting of the plankton in the dark water and the strange light the sun made now. He watched his lines to see them go straight down out of sight into the water and he was happy to see so much plankton because it meant fish. The strange light the sun made in the water, now that the sun was higher, meant good weather and so did the shape of the clouds over the land. But the bird was almost out of sight now and nothing showed on the surface of the water but some patches of yellow, sun-bleached Sargasso weed and the purple, formalized, iridescent, gelatinous bladder of a Portuguese man-of-war floating close beside the boat. It turned on its side and then righted itself. It floated cheerfully as a bubble with its long deadly purple filaments trailing a yard behind it in the water.

"*Agua mala*," the man said. "You whore."

From where he swung lightly against his oars he looked down into the water and saw the tiny fish that were coloured like the trailing filaments and swam between them and under the small shade the bubble made as it drifted. They were immune to its poison. But men were not and when some of the filaments would catch on a line and rest there slimy and purple while the old man was working a fish, he would have welts and sores on his arms and hands of the sort that poison ivy or poison oak can give. But these poisonings from the *agua mala* came quickly and struck like a whiplash.

The iridescent bubbles were beautiful. But they were the falsest thing in the sea and the old man loved to see the big sea turtles eating them. The turtles saw them, approached them from the front, then shut their eyes so they were completely carapaced and ate them filaments and all. The old man loved to see the turtles eat them and he loved to walk on them on the beach after a storm and hear them pop when he stepped on them with the horny soles of his feet.

He loved green turtles and hawk-bills with their elegance and speed and their great value and he had a friendly contempt for the huge, stupid loggerheads, yellow in their armour-plating, strange in their love-making, and happily eating the Portuguese men-of-war with their eyes shut.

He had no mysticism about turtles although he had gone in turtle boats for many years. He was sorry for them all, even the great trunk backs that were as long as the skiff and weighed a ton. Most people are heartless about turtles because a turtle's heart will beat for hours after he has been cut up and butchered. But the old man thought, I have such a heart too and my feet and hands are like theirs. He ate the white eggs to give himself strength. He ate them all through May to be strong in September and October for the truly big fish.

He also drank a cup of shark liver oil each day from the big drum in the shack where many of the fishermen kept their gear. It was there for all fishermen who wanted it. Most fishermen hated the taste. But it was no worse than getting up at the hours that they rose and it was very good against all colds and grippes and it was good for the eyes.

Now the old man looked up and saw that the bird was circling again.

"He's found fish," he said aloud. No flying fish broke the surface and there was no scattering of bait fish. But as the old man watched, a small tuna rose in the air, turned and dropped head first into the water. The tuna shone silver in the sun and after he had dropped back into the water another and another rose and they were jumping in all directions, churning the water and leaping in long jumps after the bait. They were circling it and driving it.

If they don't travel too fast I will get into them, the old man thought, and he watched the school working the water white and the bird now dropping and dipping into the bait fish that were forced to the surface in their panic.

"The bird is a great help," the old man said. Just then the stern line came taut under his foot, where he had kept a loop of the line, and he dropped his oars and felt the weight of the small tuna's shivering pull as he held the line firm and commenced to haul it in. The shivering increased as he pulled in and he could see the blue back of the fish in the water and the gold of his sides before he swung him over the side and into the boat. He lay in the stern in the sun, compact and bullet shaped, his big, unintelligent eyes staring as he thumped his life out against the planking of the boat with the quick shivering strokes of his neat, fast-moving tail. The old man hit him on the head for kindness and kicked him, his body still shuddering, under the shade of the stern.

"Albacore," he said aloud. "He'll make a beautiful bait. He'll weigh ten pounds."

He did not remember when he had first started to talk aloud when he was by himself. He had sung when he was by himself in the old days and he had sung at night sometimes when he was alone steering on his watch in the smacks or in the turtle boats. He had probably started to talk aloud, when alone, when the boy had left. But he did not remember. When he and the boy fished together they usually spoke only when it was necessary. They talked at night or when they were storm-bound by bad weather. It was considered a virtue not to talk unnecessarily at sea and the old man had always considered it so and respected it. But now he said his thoughts aloud many times since there was no one that they could annoy.

"If the others heard me talking out loud they would think that I am crazy," he said aloud. "But since I am not crazy, I do not care. And the rich have radios to talk to them in their boats and to bring them the baseball."

Now is no time to think of baseball, he thought. Now is the time to think of only one thing. That which I was born for. There might be a big one around that school, he thought. I picked up only a straggler from the albacore that were feeding. But they are working far out and fast. Everything that shows on the surface today travels very fast and to the north-east. Can that be the time of day? Or is it some sign of weather that I do not know?

He could not see the green of the shore now but only the tops of the blue hills that showed white as though they were snow-capped and the clouds that looked like high snow mountains above them. The sea was very dark and the light made prisms in the water. The myriad flecks of the plankton were annulled now by the high sun and it was only the great deep prisms in the blue water that the old man saw now with his lines going straight down into the water that was a mile deep.

The tuna, the fishermen called all the fish of that species tuna and only distinguished among them by their proper names when they came to sell them or to trade them for baits, were down again. The sun was hot now and the old man felt it on the back of his neck and felt the sweat trickle down his back as he rowed.

I could just drift, he thought, and sleep and put a bight of line around my toe to wake me. But today is eighty-five days and I should fish the day well.

Just then, watching his lines, he saw one of the projecting green sticks dip sharply.

"Yes," he said. "Yes," and shipped his oars without bumping the boat. He reached out for the line and held it softly between the thumb and forefinger of his right hand. He felt no strain nor weight and he held the line lightly. Then it came again. This time it was a tentative pull, not solid nor heavy, and he knew exactly what it was. One hundred fathoms down a marlin was eating the sardines that covered the point and the shank of the hook where the hand-forged hook projected from the head of the small tuna.

The old man held the line delicately, and softly, with his left hand, unleashed it from the stick. Now he could let it run through his fingers without the fish feeling any tension.

This far out, he must be huge in this month, he thought. Eat them, fish. Eat them. Please eat them. How fresh they are and you down there six hundred feet in that cold water in the dark. Make another turn in the dark and come back and eat them.

He felt the light delicate pulling and then a harder pull when a sardine's head must have been more difficult to break from the hook. Then there was nothing.

"Come on," the old man said aloud. "Make another turn. Just smell them. Aren't they lovely? Eat them good now and then there is the tuna. Hard and cold and lovely. Don't be shy, fish. Eat them."

He waited with the line between his thumb and his finger, watching it and the other lines at the same time for the fish might have swum up or down. Then came the same delicate pulling touch again.

"He'll take it," the old man said aloud. "God help him to take it."

He did not take it though. He was gone and the old man felt nothing.

"He can't have gone," he said. "Christ knows he can't have gone. He's making a turn. Maybe he has been hooked before and he remembers something of it."

Then he felt the gentle touch on the line and he was happy.

"It was only his turn," he said. "He'll take it."

He was happy feeling the gentle pulling and then he felt something hard and unbelievably heavy. It was the weight of the fish and he let the line slip down, down, down, unrolling off the first of the two reserve coils. As it went down, slipping lightly through the old man's fingers, he still could feel the great weight, though the pressure of his thumb and finger were almost imperceptible.

"What a fish," he said. "He has it sideways in his mouth now and he is moving off with it."

Then he will turn and swallow it, he thought. He did not say that because he knew that if you said a good thing it might not happen. He knew what a huge fish this was and he thought of him moving away in the darkness with the tuna held crosswise in his mouth. At that moment he felt him stop moving but the weight was still there. Then the weight increased and he gave more line. He tightened the pressure of his thumb and finger for a moment and the weight increased and was going straight down.

"He's taken it," he said. "Now I'll let him eat it well."

He let the line slip through his fingers while he reached down with his left hand and made fast the free end of the two reserve coils to the loop of the two reserve coils of the next line. Now he was ready. He had three forty-fathom coils of line in reserve now, as well as the coil he was using.

"Eat it a little more," he said. "Eat it well."

Eat it so that the point of the hook goes into your heart and kills you, he thought. Come up easy and let me put the harpoon into you. All right. Are you ready? Have you been long enough at table?

"Now!" he said aloud and struck hard with both hands, gained a yard of line and then struck again and again, swinging with each arm alternately on the cord with all the strength of his arms and the pivoted weight of his body.

Nothing happened. The fish just moved away slowly and the old man could not raise him an inch. His line was strong and made for heavy fish and he held it against his back until it was so taut that beads of water were jumping from it. Then it began to make a slow hissing sound in the water and he still held it, bracing himself against the thwart and leaning back against the pull. The boat began to move slowly off toward the north-west.

The fish moved steadily and they travelled slowly on

the calm water. The other baits were still in the water but there was nothing to be done.

"I wish I had the boy," the old man said aloud. "I'm being towed by a fish and I'm the towing bitt. I could make the line fast. But then he could break it. I must hold him all I can and give him line when he must have it. Thank God he is travelling and not going down."

What I will do if he decides to go down, I don't know. What I'll do if he sounds and dies I don't know. But I'll do something. There are plenty of things I can do.

He held the line against his back and watched its slant in the water and the skiff moving steadily to the northwest.

This will kill him, the old man thought. He can't do this forever. But four hours later the fish was still swimming steadily out to sea, towing the skiff, and the old man was still braced solidly with the line across his back.

"It was noon when I hooked him," he said. "And I have never seen him."

He had pushed his straw hat hard down on his head before he hooked the fish and it was cutting his forehead. He was thirsty too and he got down on his knees and, being careful not to jerk on the line, moved as far into the bow as he could get and reached the water bottle with one hand. He opened it and drank a little. Then he rested against the bow. He rested sitting on the un-stepped mast and sail and tried not to think but only to endure.

Then he looked behind him and saw that no land was visible. That makes no difference, he thought. I can always come in on the glow from Havana. There are two more hours before the sun sets and maybe he will come up before that. If he doesn't maybe he will come up with the moon.

If he does not do that maybe he will come up with the sunrise. I have no cramps and I feel strong. It is he that has the hook in his mouth. But what a fish to pull like that. He must have his mouth shut tight on the wire. I wish I could see him. I wish I could see him only once to know what I have against me.

The fish never changed his course nor his direction all that night as far as the man could tell from watching the stars. It was cold after the sun went down and the old man's sweat dried cold on his back and his arms and his old legs. During the day he had taken the sack that covered the bait box and spread it in the sun to dry. After the sun went down he tied it around his neck so that it hung down over his back and he cautiously worked it down under the line that was across his shoulders now. The sack cushioned the line and he had found a way of leaning forward against the bow so that he was almost comfortable. The position actually was only somewhat less intolerable; but he thought of it as almost comfortable.

I can do nothing with him and he can do nothing with me, he thought. Not as long as he keeps this up.

Once he stood up and urinated over the side of the skiff and looked at the stars and checked his course. The line showed like a phosphorescent streak in the water straight out from his shoulders. They were moving more slowly now and the glow of Havana was not so strong, so that he knew the current must be carrying them to the eastward. If I lose the glare of Havana we must be going more to the eastward, he thought. For if the fish's course held true I must see it for many more hours. I wonder how the baseball came out in the grand leagues today, he thought. It would be wonderful to do this with a radio.

Then he thought, think of it always. Think of what you are doing. You must do nothing stupid.

Then he said aloud, "I wish I had the boy. To help me and to see this."

No one should be alone in their old age, he thought. But it is unavoidable. I must remember to eat the tuna before he spoils in order to keep strong. Remember, no matter how little you want to, that you must eat him in the morning. Remember, he said to himself.

During the night two porpoises came around the boat and he could hear them rolling and blowing. He could tell the difference between the blowing noise the male made and the sighing blow of the female.

"They are good," he said. "They play and make jokes and love one another. They are our brothers like the flying fish."

Then he began to pity the great fish that he had hooked. He is wonderful and strange and who knows how old he is, he thought. Never have I had such a strong fish nor one who acted so strangely. Perhaps he is too wise to jump. He could ruin me by jumping or by a wild rush. But perhaps he has been hooked many times before and he knows that this is how he should make his fight. He cannot know that it is only one man against him, nor that it is an old man. But what a great fish he is and what he will bring in the market if the flesh is good. He took the bait like a male and he pulls like a male and his fight has no panic in it. I wonder if he has any plans or if he is just as desperate as I am?

He remembered the time he had hooked one of a pair of marlin. The male fish always let the female fish feed first and the hooked fish, the female, made a wild, panic-stricken, despairing fight that soon exhausted her, and all the time the male had stayed with her, crossing the line and circling with her on the surface. He had stayed so close that the old man was afraid he would cut the line with his tail which was sharp as a scythe and almost of that size and shape. When the old man had gaffed her and clubbed her, holding the rapier bill with its sandpaper edge and clubbing her across the top of her head until her colour turned to a colour almost like the backing of mirrors, and then, with the boy's aid, hoisted her aboard, the male fish had stayed by the side of the boat. Then, while the old man was clearing the lines and preparing the harpoon, the male fish jumped high into the air beside the boat to see where the female was and then went down deep, his lavender wings, that were his pectoral fins, spread wide and all his wide lavender stripes showing. He was beautiful, the old man remembered, and he had stayed.

That was the saddest thing I ever saw with them, the old man thought. The boy was sad too and we begged her pardon and butchered her promptly.

"I wish the boy was here," he said aloud and settled himself against the rounded planks of the bow and felt the strength of the great fish through the line he held across his shoulders moving steadily toward whatever he had chosen.

When once, through my treachery, it had been necessary to him to make a choice, the old man thought.

His choice had been to stay in the deep dark water far out beyond all snares and traps and treacheries. My choice was to go there to find him beyond all people. Beyond all people in the world. Now we are joined together and have been since noon. And no one to help either one of us.

Perhaps I should not have been a fisherman, he thought.

But that was the thing that I was born for. I must surely remember to eat the tuna after it gets light.

Some time before daylight something took one of the baits that were behind him. He heard the stick break and the line begin to rush out over the gunwale of the skiff. In the darkness he loosened his sheath knife and taking all the strain of the fish on his left shoulder he leaned back and cut the line against the wood of the gunwale. Then he cut the other line closest to him and in the dark made the loose ends of the reserve coils fast. He worked skillfully with the one hand and put his foot on the coils to hold them as he drew his knots tight. Now he had six reserve coils of line. There were two from each bait he had severed and the two from the bait the fish had taken and they were all connected.

After it is light, he thought, I will work back to the forty-fathom bait and cut it away too and link up the reserve coils. I will have lost two hundred fathoms of good Catalan *cardel* and the hooks and leaders. That can be replaced. But who replaces this fish if I hook some fish and it cuts him off? I don't know what that fish was that took the bait just now. It could have been a marlin or a broadbill or a shark. I never felt him. I had to get rid of him too fast.

Aloud he said, "I wish I had the boy."

But you haven't got the boy, he thought. You have only yourself and you had better work back to the last line now, in the dark or not in the dark, and cut it away and hook up the two reserve coils.

So he did it. It was difficult in the dark and once the fish made a surge that pulled him down on his face and made a cut below his eye. The blood ran down his cheek a little way. But it coagulated and dried before it reached his chin and he worked his way back to the bow and rested against the wood. He adjusted the sack and carefully worked the line so that it came across a new part of his shoulders and, holding it anchored with his shoulders, he carefully felt the pull of the fish and then felt with his hand the progress of the skiff through the water.

I wonder what he made that lurch for, he thought. The wire must have slipped on the great hill of his back. Certainly his back cannot feel as badly as mine does. But he cannot pull this skiff forever, no matter how great he is. Now everything is cleared away that might make trouble and I have a big reserve of line; all that a man can ask.

"Fish," he said softly, aloud, "I'll stay with you until I am dead."

He'll stay with me too, I suppose, the old man thought and he waited for it to be light. It was cold now in the time before daylight and he pushed against the wood to be warm. I can do it as long as he can, he thought. And in the first light the line extended out and down into the water. The boat moved steadily and when the first edge of the sun rose it was on the old man's right shoulder.

"He's headed north," the old man said. The current will have set us far to the eastward, he thought. I wish he would turn with the current. That would show that he was tiring.

When the sun had risen further the old man realized that the fish was not tiring. There was only one favorable sign. The slant of the line showed he was swimming at a lesser depth. That did not necessarily mean that he would jump. But he might.

"God let him jump," the old man said. "I have enough line to handle him."

Maybe if I can increase the tension just a little it will

hurt him and he will jump, he thought. Now that it is daylight let him jump so that he'll fill the sacks along his backbone with air and then he cannot go deep to die.

He tried to increase the tension, but the line had been taut up to the very edge of the breaking point since he had hooked the fish and he felt the harshness as he leaned back to pull and knew he could put no more strain on it. I must not jerk it ever, he thought. Each jerk widens the cut the hook makes and then when he does jump he might throw it. Anyway I feel better with the sun and for once I do not have to look into it.

There was yellow weed on the line but the old man knew that only made an added drag and he was pleased. It was the yellow Gulf weed that had made so much phosphorescence in the night.

"Fish," he said, "I love you and respect you very much. But I will kill you dead before this day ends."

Let us hope so, he thought.

A small bird came toward the skiff from the north. He was a warbler and flying very low over the water. The old man could see that he was very tired.

The bird made the stern of the boat and rested there. Then he flew around the old man's head and rested on the line where he was more comfortable.

"How old are you?" the old man asked the bird. "Is this your first trip?"

The bird looked at him when he spoke. He was too tired even to examine the line and he teetered on it as his delicate feet gripped it fast.

"It's steady," the old man told him. "It's too steady. You shouldn't be that tired after a windless night. What are birds coming to?"

The hawks, he thought, that come out to sea to meet them. But he said nothing of this to the bird who could not understand him anyway and who would learn about the hawks soon enough.

"Take a good rest, small bird," he said. "Then go in and take your chance like any man or bird or fish."

It encouraged him to talk because his back had stiffened in the night and it hurt truly now.

"Stay at my house if you like, bird," he said. "I am sorry I cannot hoist the sail and take you in with the small breeze that is rising. But I am with a friend."

Just then the fish gave a sudden lurch that pulled the old man down onto the bow and would have pulled him overboard if he had not braced himself and given some line.

The bird had flown up when the line jerked and the old man had not even seen him go. He felt the line carefully with his right hand and noticed his hand was bleeding.

"Something hurt him then," he said aloud and pulled back on the line to see if he could turn the fish. But when he was touching the breaking point he held steady and settled back against the strain of the line.

"You're feeling it now, fish," he said. "And so, God knows, am I."

He looked around for the bird now because he would have liked him for company. The bird was gone.

You did not stay long, the man thought. But it is rougher where you are going until you make the shore. How did I let the fish cut me with that one quick pull he made? I must be getting very stupid. Or perhaps I was looking at the small bird and thinking of him. Now I will pay attention to my work and then I must eat the tuna so that I will not have a failure of strength.

"I wish the boy were here and that I had some salt," he said aloud.

Shifting the weight of the line to his left shoulder and kneeling carefully he washed his hand in the ocean and held it there, submerged, for more than a minute watching the blood trail away and the steady movement of the water against his hand as the boat moved.

"He has slowed much," he said.

The old man would have liked to keep his hand in the salt water longer but he was afraid of another sudden lurch by the fish and he stood up and braced himself and held his hand up against the sun. It was only a line burn that had cut his flesh. But it was in the working part of his hand. He knew he would need his hands before this was over and he did not like to be cut before it started.

"Now," he said, when his hand had dried, "I must eat the small tuna. I can reach him with the gaff and eat him here in comfort."

He knelt down and found the tuna under the stern with the gaff and drew it toward him keeping it clear of the coiled lines. Holding the line with his left shoulder again, and bracing on his left hand and arm, he took the tuna off the gaff hook and put the gaff back in place. He put one knee on the fish and cut strips of dark red meat longitudinally from the back of the head to the tail. They were wedge-shaped strips and he cut them from next to the backbone down to the edge of the belly. When he had cut six strips he spread them out on the wood of the bow, wiped his knife on his trousers, and lifted the carcass of the bonito by the tail and dropped it overboard.

"I don't think I can eat an entire one," he said and drew his knife across one of the strips. He could feel the steady hard pull of the line and his left hand was cramped. It drew up tight on the heavy cord and he looked at it in disgust.

"What kind of a hand is that," he said. "Cramp then if you want. Make yourself into a claw. It will do you no good."

Come on, he thought and looked down into the dark water at the slant of the line. Eat it now and it will strengthen the hand. It is not the hand's fault and you have been many hours with the fish. But you can stay with him forever. Eat the bonito now.

He picked up a piece and put it in his mouth and chewed it slowly. It was not unpleasant.

Chew it well, he thought, and get all the juices. It would not be bad to eat with a little lime or with lemon or with salt.

"How do you feel, hand?" he asked the cramped hand that was almost as stiff as rigor mortis. "I'll eat some more for you."

He ate the other part of the piece that he had cut in two. He chewed it carefully and then spat out the skin.

"How does it go, hand? Or is it too early to know?"

He took another full piece and chewed it.

"It is a strong full-blooded fish," he thought. "I was lucky to get him instead of dolphin. Dolphin is too sweet. This is hardly sweet at all and all the strength is still in it."

There is no sense in being anything but practical though, he thought. I wish I had some salt. And I do not know whether the sun will rot or dry what is left, so I had better eat it all although I am not hungry. The fish is calm and steady. I will eat it all and then I will be ready.

"Be patient, hand," he said. "I do this for you."

I wish I could feed the fish, he thought. He is my

brother. But I must kill him and keep strong to do it. Slowly and conscientiously he ate all of the wedge-shaped strips of fish.

He straightened up, wiping his hand on his trousers.

"Now," he said. "You can let the cord go, hand, and I will handle him with the right arm alone until you stop that nonsense." He put his left foot on the heavy line that the left hand had held and lay back against the pull against his back.

"God help me to have the cramp go," he said. "Because I do not know what the fish is going to do."

But he seems calm, he thought, and following his plan. But what is his plan, he thought. And what is mine? Mine I must improvise to his because of his great size. If he will jump I can kill him. But he stays down forever. Then I will stay down with him forever.

He rubbed the cramped hand against his trousers and tried to gentle the fingers. But it would not open. Maybe it will open with the sun, he thought. Maybe it will open when the strong raw tuna is digested. If I have to have it, I will open it, cost whatever it costs. But I do not want to open it now by force. Let it open by itself and come back of its own accord. After all I abused it much in the night when it was necessary to free and untie the various lines.

He looked across the sea and knew how alone he was now. But he could see the prisms in the deep dark water and the line stretching ahead and the strange undulation of the calm. The clouds were building up now for the trade wind and he looked ahead and saw a flight of wild ducks etching themselves against the sky over the water, then blurring, then etching again and he knew no man was ever alone on the sea.

He thought of how some men feared being out of sight of land in a small boat and knew they were right in the months of sudden bad weather. But now they were in hurricane months and, when there are no hurricanes, the weather of hurricane months is the best of all the year.

If there is a hurricane you always see the signs of it in the sky for days ahead, if you are at sea. They do not see it ashore because they do not know what to look for, he thought. The land must make a difference too, in the shape of the clouds. But we have no hurricane coming now.

He looked at the sky and saw the white cumulus built like friendly piles of ice cream and high above were the thin feathers of the cirrus against the high September sky.

"Light *brisa*," he said. "Better weather for me than for you, fish."

His left hand was still cramped, but he was unknotting it slowly.

I hate a cramp, he thought. It is a treachery of one's own body. It is humiliating before others to have a diarrhoea from ptomaine poisoning or to vomit from it. But a cramp, he thought of it as a *calambre*, humiliates oneself especially when one is alone.

If the boy were here he could rub it for me and loosen it down from the forearm, he thought. But it will loosen up.

Then, with his right hand he felt the difference in the pull of the line before he saw the slant change in the water. Then, as he leaned against the line and slapped his left hand hard and fast against his thigh he saw the line slanting slowly upward.

"He's coming up," he said. "Come on hand. Please come on."

The line rose slowly and steadily and then the surface

of the ocean bulged ahead of the boat and the fish came out. He came out unendingly and water poured from his sides. He was bright in the sun and his head and back were dark purple and in the sun the stripes on his sides showed wide and a light lavender. His sword was as long as a baseball bat and tapered like a rapier and he rose his full length from the water and then re-entered it, smoothly, like a diver and the old man saw the great scythe-blade of his tail go under and the line commenced to race out.

"He is two feet longer than the skiff," the old man said. The line was going out fast but steadily and the fish was not panicked. The old man was trying with both hands to keep the line just inside of breaking strength. He knew that if he could not slow the fish with a steady pressure the fish could take out all the line and break it.

He is a great fish and I must convince him, he thought. I must never let him learn his strength nor what he could do if he made his run. If I were him I would put in everything now and go until something broke. But, thank God, they are not as intelligent as we who kill them; although they are more noble and more able.

The old man had seen many great fish. He had seen many that weighed more than a thousand pounds and he had caught two of that size in his life, but never alone. Now alone, and out of sight of land, he was fast to the biggest fish that he had ever seen and bigger than he had ever heard of, and his left hand was still as tight as the gripped claws of an eagle.

It will uncramp though, he thought. Surely it will uncramp to help my right hand. There are three things that are brothers: the fish and my two hands. It must uncramp.

It is unworthy of it to be cramped. The fish had slowed again and was going at his usual pace.

I wonder why he jumped, the old man thought. He jumped almost as though to show me how big he was. I know now, anyway, he thought. I wish I could show him what sort of man I am. But then he would see the cramped hand. Let him think I am more man than I am and I will be so. I wish I was the fish, he thought, with everything he has against only my will and my intelligence.

He settled comfortably against the wood and took his suffering as it came and the fish swam steadily and the boat moved slowly through the dark water. There was a small sea rising with the wind coming up from the east and at noon the old man's left hand was uncramped.

"Bad news for you, fish," he said and shifted the line over the sacks that covered his shoulders.

He was comfortable but suffering, although he did not admit the suffering at all.

"I am not religious," he said. "But I will say ten Our Fathers and ten Hail Marys that I should catch this fish, and I promise to make a pilgrimage to the Virgin of Cobre if I catch him. That is a promise."

He commenced to say his prayers mechanically. Sometimes he would be so tired that he could not remember the prayer and then he would say them fast so that they would come automatically. Hail Marys are easier to say than Our Fathers, he thought.

"Hail Mary full of Grace the Lord is with thee. Blessed art thou among women and blessed is the fruit of thy womb, Jesus. Holy Mary, Mother of God, pray for us sinners now and at the hour of our death. Amen." Then he added, "Blessed Virgin, pray for the death of this fish. Wonderful though he is."

With his prayers said, and feeling much better, but suffering exactly as much, and perhaps a little more, he leaned against the wood of the bow and began, mechanically, to work the fingers of his left hand.

The sun was hot now although the breeze was rising gently.

"I had better re-bait that little line out over the stern," he said. "If the fish decides to stay another night I will need to eat again and the water is low in the bottle. I don't think I can get anything but a dolphin here. But if I eat him fresh enough he won't be bad. I wish a flying fish would come on board tonight. But I have no light to attract them. A flying fish is excellent to eat raw and I would not have to cut him up. I must save all my strength now. Christ, I did not know he was so big."

"I'll kill him though," he said. "In all his greatness and his glory."

Although it is unjust, he thought. But I will show him what a man can do and what a man endures.

"I told the boy I was a strange old man," he said. "Now is when I must prove it."

The thousand times that he had proved it meant nothing. Now he was proving it again. Each time was a new time and he never thought about the past when he was doing it.

I wish he'd sleep and I could sleep and dream about the lions, he thought. Why are the lions the main thing that is left? Don't think, old man, he said to himself. Rest gently now against the wood and think of nothing. He is working. Work as little as you can.

It was getting into the afternoon and the boat still moved slowly and steadily. But there was an added drag now from the easterly breeze and the old man rode gently with the small sea and the hurt of the cord across his back came to him easily and smoothly.

Once in the afternoon the line started to rise again. But the fish only continued to swim at a slightly higher level. The sun was on the old man's left arm and shoulder and on his back. So he knew the fish had turned east of north.

Now that he had seen him once, he could picture the fish swimming in the water with his purple pectoral fins set wide as wings and the great erect tail slicing through the dark. I wonder how much he sees at that depth, the old man thought. His eye is huge and a horse, with much less eye, can see in the dark. Once I could see quite well in the dark. Not in the absolute dark. But almost as a cat sees.

The sun and his steady movement of his fingers had uncramped his left hand now completely and he began to shift more of the strain to it and he shrugged the muscles of his back to shift the hurt of the cord a little.

"If you're not tired, fish," he said aloud, "you must be very strange."

He felt very tired now and he knew the night would come soon and he tried to think of other things. He thought of the Big Leagues, to him they were the *Gran Ligas*, and he knew that the Yankees of New York were playing the *Tigres* of Detroit.

This is the second day now that I do not know the result of the *juegos*, he thought. But I must have confidence and I must be worthy of the great DiMaggio who does all things perfectly even with the pain of the bone spur in his heel. What is a bone spur? he asked himself. *Un espuela de hueso*. We do not have them. Can it be as painful as the spur of a fighting cock in one's heel? I do not think I could endure that or the loss of the eye and of both eyes and continue to fight as the fighting cocks do. Man is not much beside the great birds and beasts. Still I would rather be that beast down there in the darkness of the sea.

"Unless sharks come," he said aloud. "If sharks come, God pity him and me."

Do you believe the great DiMaggio would stay with a fish as long as I will stay with this one? he thought. I am sure he would and more since he is young and strong. Also his father was a fisherman. But would the bone spur hurt him too much?

"I do not know," he said aloud. "I never had a bone spur."

As the sun set he remembered, to give himself more confidence, the time in the tavern at Casablanca when he had played the hand game with the great negro from Cienfuegos who was the strongest man on the docks. They had gone one day and one night with their elbows on a chalk line on the table and their forearms straight up and their hands gripped tight. Each one was trying to force the other's hand down onto the table. There was much betting and people went in and out of the room under the kerosene lights and he had looked at the arm and hand of the negro and at the negro's face. They changed the referees every four hours after the first eight so that the referees could sleep. Blood came out from under the fingernails of both his and the negro's hands and they looked each other in the eye and at their hands and forearms and the bettors went in and out of the room and sat on high chairs against the wall and watched. The walls were painted bright blue and were of wood and the lamps threw their shadows against them. The negro's shadow was huge and it moved on the wall as the breeze moved the lamps.

The odds would change back and forth all night and they fed the negro rum and lighted cigarettes for him. Then the negro, after the rum, would try for a tremendous effort and once he had the old man, who was not an old man then but was Santiago *El Campeón*, nearly three inches off balance. But the old man had raised his hand up to dead even again. He was sure then that he had the negro, who was a fine man and a great athlete, beaten. And at daylight when the bettors were asking that it be called a draw and the referee was shaking his head, he had unleashed his effort and forced the hand of the negro down and down until it rested on the wood. The match had started on a Sunday morning and ended on a Monday morning. Many of the bettors had asked for a draw because they had to go to work on the docks loading sacks of sugar or at the Havana Coal Company. Otherwise everyone would have wanted it to go to a finish. But he had finished it anyway and before anyone had to go to work.

For a long time after that everyone had called him The Champion and there had been a return match in the spring. But not much money was bet and he had won it quite easily since he had broken the confidence of the negro from Cienfuegos in the first match. After that he had a few matches and then no more. He decided that he could beat anyone if he wanted to badly enough and he decided that it was bad for his right hand for fishing. He had tried a few practice matches with his left hand. But his left hand had always been a traitor and would not do what he called on it to do and he did not trust it.

The sun will bake it out well now, he thought. It should not cramp on me again unless it gets too cold in the night. I wonder what this night will bring.

An airplane passed overhead on its course to Miami and he watched its shadow scaring up the schools of flying fish.

"With so much flying fish there should be dolphin," he said, and leaned back on the line to see if it was possible to gain any on his fish. But he could not and it stayed at the hardness and water-drop shivering that preceded breaking. The boat moved ahead slowly and he watched the airplane until he could no longer see it.

It must be very strange in an airplane, he thought. I wonder what the sea looks like from that height? They should be able to see the fish well if they do not fly too high. I would like to fly very slowly at two hundred fathoms high and see the fish from above. In the turtle boats I was in the cross-trees of the mast-head and even at that height I saw much. The dolphin look greener from there and you can see their stripes and their purple spots and you can see all of the school as they swim. Why is it that all the fast-moving fish of the dark current have purple backs and usually purple stripes or spots? The dolphin looks green of course because he is really golden. But when he comes to feed, truly hungry, purple stripes show on his sides as on a marlin. Can it be anger, or the greater speed he makes that brings them out?

Just before it was dark, as they passed a great island of Sargasso weed that heaved and swung in the light sea as though the ocean were making love with something under a yellow blanket, his small line was taken by a dolphin. He saw it first when it jumped in the air, true gold in the last of the sun and bending and flapping wildly in the air. It jumped again and again in the acrobatics of its fear and he worked his way back to the stern and crouching and holding the big line with his right hand and arm, he pulled the dolphin in with his left hand, stepping on the gained line each time with his bare left foot. When the fish was at the stern, plunging and cutting from side to side in desperation, the old man leaned over the stern and lifted the burnished gold fish with its purple spots over the stern. Its jaws were working convulsively in quick bites against the hook and it pounded the bottom of the skiff with its long flat body, its tail and its head until he clubbed it across the shining golden head until it shivered and was still.

The old man unhooked the fish, re-baited the line with another sardine and tossed it over. Then he worked his way slowly back to the bow. He washed his left hand and wiped it on his trousers. Then he shifted the heavy line from his right hand to his left and washed his right hand in the sea while he watched the sun go into the ocean and the slant of the big cord.

"He hasn't changed at all," he said. But watching the movement of the water against his hand he noted that it was perceptibly slower.

"I'll lash the two oars together across the stern and that will slow him in the night," he said. "He's good for the night and so am I."

It would be better to gut the dolphin a little later to save the blood in the meat, he thought. I can do that a little later and lash the oars to make a drag at the same time. I had better keep the fish quiet now and not disturb him too much at sunset. The setting of the sun is a difficult time for all fish.

He let his hand dry in the air then grasped the line with it and eased himself as much as he could and allowed himself to be pulled forward against the wood so that the boat took the strain as much, or more, than he did.

I'm learning how to do it, he thought. This part of it anyway. Then too, remember he hasn't eaten since he took the bait and he is huge and needs much food. I have eaten the whole bonito. Tomorrow I will eat the dolphin. He called it *dorado*. Perhaps I should eat some of it when I clean it. It will be harder to eat than the bonito. But, then, nothing is easy.

"How do you feel, fish?" he asked aloud. "I feel good and my left hand is better and I have food for a night and a day. Pull the boat, fish."

He did not truly feel good because the pain from the cord across his back had almost passed pain and gone into a dullness that he mistrusted. But I have had worse things than that, he thought. My hand is only cut a little and the cramp is gone from the other. My legs are all right. Also now I have gained on him in the question of sustenance.

It was dark now as it becomes dark quickly after the sun sets in September. He lay against the worn wood of the bow and rested all that he could. The first stars were out. He did not know the name of Rigel but he saw it and knew soon they would all be out and he would have all his distant friends.

"The fish is my friend too," he said aloud. "I have never seen or heard of such a fish. But I must kill him. I am glad we do not have to try to kill the stars."

Imagine if each day a man must try to kill the moon, he thought. The moon runs away. But imagine if a man each day should have to try to kill the sun? We were born lucky, he thought.

Then he was sorry for the great fish that had nothing to eat and his determination to kill him never relaxed in his sorrow for him. How many people will he feed, he thought. But are they worthy to eat him? No, of course not. There is no one worthy of eating him from the manner of his behaviour and his great dignity.

I do not understand these things, he thought. But it is good that we do not have to try to kill the sun or the moon or the stars. It is enough to live on the sea and kill our true brothers.

Now, he thought, I must think about the drag. It has its perils and its merits. I may lose so much line that I will lose him, if he makes his effort and the drag made by the oars is in place and the boat loses all her lightness. Her lightness prolongs both our suffering but it is my safety since he has great speed that he has never yet employed. No matter what passes I must gut the dolphin so he does not spoil and eat some of him to be strong.

Now I will rest an hour more and feel that he is solid and steady before I move back to the stern to do the work and make the decision. In the meantime I can see how he acts and if he shows any changes. The oars are a good trick; but it has reached the time to play for safety. He is much fish still and I saw that the hook was in the corner of his mouth and he has kept his mouth tight shut. The punishment of the hook is nothing. The punishment of hunger, and that he is against something that he does not comprehend, is everything. Rest now, old man, and let him work until your next duty comes.

He rested for what he believed to be two hours. The

moon did not rise now until late and he had no way of judging the time. Nor was he really resting except comparatively. He was still bearing the pull of the fish across his shoulders but he placed his left hand on the gunwale of the bow and confided more and more of the resistance to the fish to the skiff itself.

How simple it would be if I could make the line fast, he thought. But with one small lurch he could break it. I must cushion the pull of the line with my body and at all times be ready to give line with both hands.

"But you have not slept yet, old man," he said aloud. "It is half a day and a night and now another day and you have not slept. You must devise a way so that you sleep a little if he is quiet and steady. If you do not sleep you might become unclear in the head."

I'm clear enough in the head, he thought. Too clear. I am as clear as the stars that are my brothers. Still I must sleep. They sleep and the moon and the sun sleep and even the ocean sleeps sometimes on certain days when there is no current and a flat calm.

But remember to sleep, he thought. Make yourself do it and devise some simple and sure way about the lines. Now go back and prepare the dolphin. It is too dangerous to rig the oars as a drag if you must sleep.

I could go without sleeping, he told himself. But it would be too dangerous.

He started to work his way back to the stern on his hands and knees, being careful not to jerk against the fish. He may be half asleep himself, he thought. But I do not want him to rest. He must pull until he dies.

Back in the stern he turned so that his left hand held the strain of the line across his shoulders and drew his knife from its sheath with his right hand. The stars were bright now and he saw the dolphin clearly and he pushed the blade of his knife into his head and drew him out from under the stern. He put one of his feet on the fish and slit him quickly from the vent up to the tip of his lower jaw. Then he put his knife down and gutted him with his right hand, scooping him clean and pulling the gills clear. He felt the maw heavy and slippery in his hands and he slit it open. There were two flying fish inside. They were fresh and hard and he laid them side by side and dropped the guts and the gills over the stern. They sank leaving a trail of phosphorescence in the water. The dolphin was cold and a leprous gray-white now in the starlight and the old man skinned one side of him while he held his right foot on the fish's head. Then he turned him over and skinned the other side and cut each side off from the head down to the tail.

He slid the carcass overboard and looked to see if there was any swirl in the water. But there was only the light of its slow descent. He turned then and placed the two flying fish inside the two fillets of fish and putting his knife back in its sheath, he worked his way slowly back to the bow. His back was bent with the weight of the line across it and he carried the fish in his right hand.

Back in the bow he laid the two fillets of fish out on the wood with the flying fish beside them. After that he settled the line across his shoulders in a new place and held it again with his left hand resting on the gunwale. Then he leaned over the side and washed the flying fish in the water, noting the speed of the water against his hand. His hand was phosphorescent from skinning the fish and he watched the flow of the water against it. The flow was less strong and as he rubbed the side of his hand against the planking of the skiff, particles of phosphorus floated off and drifted slowly astern.

"He is tiring or he is resting," the old man said. "Now let me get through the eating of this dolphin and get some rest and a little sleep."

Under the stars and with the night colder all the time he ate half of one of the dolphin fillets and one of the flying fish, gutted and with its head cut off.

"What an excellent fish dolphin is to eat cooked," he said. "And what a miserable fish raw. I will never go in a boat again without salt or limes."

If I had brains I would have splashed water on the bow all day and drying, it would have made salt, he thought. But then I did not hook the dolphin until almost sunset. Still it was a lack of preparation. But I have chewed it all well and I am not nauseated.

The sky was clouding over to the east and one after another the stars he knew were gone. It looked now as though he were moving into a great canyon of clouds and the wind had dropped.

"There will be bad weather in three or four days," he said. "But not tonight and not tomorrow. Rig now to get some sleep, old man, while the fish is calm and steady."

He held the line tight in his right hand and then pushed his thigh against his right hand as he leaned all his weight against the wood of the bow. Then he passed the line a little lower on his shoulders and braced his left hand on it.

My right hand can hold it as long as it is braced, he thought. If it relaxes in sleep my left hand will wake me as the line goes out. It is hard on the right hand. But he is used to punishment. Even if I sleep twenty minutes or a half an hour it is good. He lay forward cramping himself against the line with all of his body, putting all his weight onto his right hand, and he was asleep.

He did not dream of the lions but instead of a vast school of porpoises that stretched for eight or ten miles and it was in the time of their mating and they would leap high into the air and return into the same hole they had made in the water when they leaped.

Then he dreamed that he was in the village on his bed and there was a norther and he was very cold and his right arm was asleep because his head had rested on it instead of a pillow.

After that he began to dream of the long yellow beach and he saw the first of the lions come down onto it in the early dark and then the other lions came and he rested his chin on the wood of the bows where the ship lay anchored with the evening off-shore breeze and he waited to see if there would be more lions and he was happy.

The moon had been up for a long time but he slept on and the fish pulled on steadily and the boat moved into the tunnel of clouds.

He woke with the jerk of his right fist coming up against his face and the line burning out through his right hand. He had no feeling of his left hand but he braked all he could with his right and the line rushed out. Finally his left hand found the line and he leaned back against the line and now it burned his back and his left hand, and his left hand was taking all the strain and cutting badly. He looked back at the coils of line and they were feeding smoothly. Just then the fish jumped making a great bursting of the ocean and then a heavy fall. Then he jumped again and again and the boat was going fast although line was still racing out and the old man was raising the strain to breaking point and raising it to breaking point again and again. He had been pulled down tight onto the bow and his face was in the cut slice of dolphin and he could not move.

This is what we waited for, he thought. So now let us take it.

Make him pay for the line, he thought. Make him pay for it.

He could not see the fish's jumps but only heard the breaking of the ocean and the heavy splash as he fell. The speed of the line was cutting his hands badly but he had always known this would happen and he tried to keep the cutting across the calloused parts and not let the line slip into the palm nor cut the fingers.

If the boy was here he would wet the coils of line, he thought. Yes. If the boy were here. If the boy were here.

The line went out and out and out but it was slowing now and he was making the fish earn each inch of it. Now he got his head up from the wood and out of the slice of fish that his cheek had crushed. Then he was on his knees and then he rose slowly to his feet. He was ceding line but more slowly all he time. He worked back to where he could feel with his foot the coils of line that he could not see. There was plenty of line still and now the fish had to pull the friction of all that new line through the water.

Yes, he thought. And now he has jumped more than a dozen times and filled the sacks along his back with air and he cannot go down deep to die where I cannot bring him up. He will start circling soon and then I must work on him. I wonder what started him so suddenly? Could it have been hunger that made him desperate, or was he frightened by something in the night? Maybe he suddenly felt fear. But he was such a calm, strong fish and he seemed so fearless and so confident. It is strange.

"You better be fearless and confident yourself, old man," he said. "You're holding him again but you cannot get line. But soon he has to circle."

The old man held him with his left hand and his shoulders now and stooped down and scooped up water in his right hand to get the crushed dolphin flesh off of his face. He was afraid that it might nauseate him and he would vomit and lose his strength. When his face was cleaned he washed his right hand in the water over the side and then let it stay in the salt water while he watched the first light come before the sunrise. He's headed almost east, he thought. That means he is tired and going with the current. Soon he will have to circle. Then our true work begins.

After he judged that his right hand had been in the water long enough he took it out and looked at it.

"It is not bad," he said. "And pain does not matter to a man."

He took hold of the line carefully so that it did not fit into any of the fresh line cuts and shifted his weight so that he could put his left hand into the sea on the other side of the skiff.

"You did not do so badly for something worthless," he said to his left hand. "But there was a moment when I could not find you."

Why was I not born with two good hands? he thought. Perhaps it was my fault in not training that one properly. But God knows he has had enough chances to learn. He did not do so badly in the night, though, and he has only cramped once. If he cramps again let the line cut him off.

When he thought that he knew that he was not being

clear-headed and he thought he should chew some more of the dolphin. But I can't, he told himself. It is better to be light-headed than to lose your strength from nausea. And I know I cannot keep it if I eat it since my face was in it. I will keep it for an emergency until it goes bad. But it is too late to try for strength now through nourishment. You're stupid, he told himself. Eat the other flying fish.

It was there, cleaned and ready, and he picked it up with his left hand and ate it chewing the bones carefully and eating all of it down to the tail.

It has more nourishment than almost any fish, he thought. At least the kind of strength that I need. Now I have done what I can, he thought. Let him begin to circle and let the fight come.

The sun was rising for the third time since he had put to sea when the fish started to circle.

He could not see by the slant of the line that the fish was circling. It was too early for that. He just felt a faint slackening of the pressure of the line and he commenced to pull on it gently with his right hand. It tightened, as always, but just when he reached the point where it would break, line began to come in. He slipped his shoulders and head from under the line and began to pull in line steadily and gently. He used both of his hands in a swinging motion and tried to do the pulling as much as he could with his body and his legs. His old legs and shoulders pivoted with the swinging of the pulling.

"It is a very big circle," he said. "But he is circling."

Then the line would not come in any more and he held it until he saw the drops jumping from it in the sun. Then it started out and the old man knelt down and let it go grudgingly back into the dark water.

"He is making the far part of his circle now," he said. I must hold all I can, he thought. The strain will shorten his circle each time. Perhaps in an hour I will see him. Now I must convince him and then I must kill him.

But the fish kept on circling slowly and the old man was wet with sweat and tired deep into his bones two hours later. But the circles were much shorter now and from the way the line slanted he could tell the fish had risen steadily while he swam.

For an hour the old man had been seeing black spots before his eyes and the sweat salted his eyes and salted the cut over his eye and on his forehead. He was not afraid of the black spots. They were normal at the tension that he was pulling on the line. Twice, though, he had felt faint and dizzy and that had worried him.

"I could not fail myself and die on a fish like this," he said. "Now that I have him coming so beautifully, God help me endure. I'll say a hundred Our Fathers and a hundred Hail Marys. But I cannot say them now."

Consider them said, he thought. I'll say them later.

Just then he felt a sudden banging and jerking on the line he held with his two hands. It was sharp and hard-feeling and heavy.

He is hitting the wire leader with his spear, he thought. That was bound to come. He had to do that. It may make him jump though and I would rather he stayed circling now. The jumps were necessary for him to take air. But after that each one can widen the opening of the hook wound and he can throw the hook.

"Don't jump, fish," he said. "Don't jump."

The fish hit the wire several times more and each time he shook his head the old man gave up a little line.

I must hold his pain where it is, he thought. Mine does not matter. I can control mine. But his pain could drive him mad.

After a while the fish stopped beating at the wire and started circling slowly again. The old man was gaining line steadily now. But he felt faint again. He lifted some sea water with his left hand and put it on his head. Then he put more on and rubbed the back of his neck.

"I have no cramps," he said. "He'll be up soon and I can last. You have to last. Don't even speak of it."

He kneeled against the bow and, for a moment, slipped the line over his back again. I'll rest now while he goes out on the circle and then stand up and work on him when he comes in, he decided.

It was a great temptation to rest in the bow and let the fish make one circle by himself without recovering any line. But when the strain showed the fish had turned to come toward the boat, the old man rose to his feet and started the pivoting and the weaving pulling that brought in all the line he gained.

I'm tireder than I have ever been, he thought, and now the trade wind is rising. But that will be good to take him in with. I need that badly.

"I'll rest on the next turn as he goes out," he said. "I feel much better. Then in two or three turns more I will have him."

His straw hat was far on the back of his head and he sank down into the bow with the pull of the line as he felt the fish turn.

You work now, fish, he thought. I'll take you at the turn.

The sea had risen considerably. But it was a fair-weather breeze and he had to have it to get home.

"I'll just steer south and west," he said. "A man is never lost at sea and it is a long island."

It was on the third turn that he saw the fish first.

He saw him first as a dark shadow that took so long to pass under the boat that he could not believe its length.

"No," he said. "He can't be that big."

But he was that big and at the end of this circle he came to the surface only thirty yards away and the man saw his tail out of water. It was higher than a big scythe blade and a very pale lavender above the dark blue water. It raked back and as the fish swam just below the surface the old man could see his huge bulk and the purple stripes that banded him. His dorsal fin was down and his huge pectorals were spread wide.

On this circle the old man could see the fish's eye and the two gray sucking fish that swam around him. Sometimes they attached themselves to him. Sometimes they darted off. Sometimes they would swim easily in his shadow. They were each over three feet long and when they swam fast they lashed their whole bodies like eels.

The old man was sweating now but from something else besides the sun. On each calm placid turn the fish made he was gaining line and he was sure that in two turns more he would have a chance to get the harpoon in.

But I must get him close, close, close, he thought. I mustn't try for the head. I must get the heart.

"Be calm and strong, old man," he said.

On the next circle the fish's back was out but he was a little too far from the boat. On the next circle he was still too far away but he was higher out of water and the old man was sure that by gaining some more line he could have him alongside.

He had rigged his harpoon long before and its coil of light rope was in a round basket and the end was made fast to the bitt in the bow.

The fish was coming in on his circle now calm and beautiful looking and only his great tail moving. The old man pulled on him all that he could to bring him closer. For just a moment the fish turned a little on his side. Then he straightened himself and began another circle.

"I moved him," the old man said. "I moved him then."

He felt faint again now but he held on the great fish all the strain that he could. I moved him, he thought. Maybe this time I can get him over. Pull, hands, he thought. Hold up, legs. Last for me, head. Last for me. You never went. This time I'll pull him over.

But when he put all of his effort on, starting it well out before the fish came alongside and pulling with all his strength, the fish pulled part way over and then righted himself and swam away.

"Fish," the old man said. "Fish, you are going to have to die anyway. Do you have to kill me too?"

That way nothing is accomplished, he thought. His mouth was too dry to speak but he could not reach for the water now. I must get him alongside this time, he thought. I am not good for many more turns. Yes you are, he told himself. You're good for ever.

On the next turn, he nearly had him. But again the fish righted himself and swam slowly away.

You are killing me, fish, the old man thought. But you have a right to. Never have I seen a greater, or more beautiful, or a calmer or more noble thing than you, brother. Come on and kill me. I do not care who kills who.

Now you are getting confused in the head, he thought.

You must keep your head clear. Keep your head clear and know how to suffer like a man. Or a fish, he thought.

"Clear up, head," he said in a voice he could hardly hear. "Clear up."

Twice more it was the same on the turns.

I do not know, the old man thought. He had been on the point of feeling himself go each time. I do not know. But I will try it once more.

He tried it once more and he felt himself going when he turned the fish. The fish righted himself and swam off again slowly with the great tail weaving in the air.

I'll try it again, the old man promised, although his hands were mushy now and he could only see well in flashes.

He tried it again and it was the same. So he thought, and he felt himself going before he started; I will try it once again.

He took all his pain and what was left of his strength and his long gone pride and he put it against the fish's agony and the fish came over onto his side and swam gently on his side, his bill almost touching the planking of the skiff and started to pass the boat, long, deep, wide, silver and barred with purple and interminable in the water.

The old man dropped the line and put his foot on it and lifted the harpoon as high as he could and drove it down with all his strength, and more strength he had just summoned, into the fish's side just behind the great chest fin that rose high in the air to the altitude of the man's chest. He felt the iron go in and he leaned on it and drove it further and then pushed all his weight after it.

Then the fish came alive, with his death in him, and rose high out of the water showing all his great length and width and all his power and his beauty. He seemed to hang in the air above the old man in the skiff. Then he fell into the water with a crash that sent spray over the old man and over all of the skiff.

The old man felt faint and sick and he could not see well. But he cleared the harpoon line and let it run slowly through his raw hands and, when he could see, he saw the fish was on his back with his silver belly up. The shaft of the harpoon was projecting at an angle from the fish's shoulder and the sea was discolouring with the red of the blood from his heart. First it was dark as a shoal in the blue water that was more than a mile deep. Then it spread like a cloud. The fish was silvery and still and floated with the waves.

The old man looked carefully in the glimpse of vision that he had. Then he took two turns of the harpoon line around the bitt in the bow and laid his head on his hands.

"Keep my head clear," he said against the wood of the bow. "I am a tired old man. But I have killed this fish which is my brother and now I must do the slave work."

Now I must prepare the nooses and the rope to lash him alongside, he thought. Even if we were two and swamped her to load him and bailed her out, this skiff would never hold him. I must prepare everything, then bring him in and lash him well and step the mast and set sail for home.

He started to pull the fish in to have him alongside so that he could pass a line through his gills and out his mouth and make his head fast alongside the bow. I want to see him, he thought, and to touch and to feel him. He is my fortune, he thought. But that is not why I wish to feel him. I think I felt his heart, he thought. When I pushed on the harpoon shaft the second time. Bring him in now and make him fast and get the noose around his tail and another around his middle to bind him to the skiff.

"Get to work, old man," he said. He took a very small drink of the water. "There is very much slave work to be done now that the fight is over."

He looked up at the sky and then out to his fish. He looked at the sun carefully. It is not much more than noon, he thought. And the trade wind is rising. The lines all mean nothing now. The boy and I will splice them when we are home.

"Come on, fish," he said. But the fish did not come. Instead he lay there wallowing now in the seas and the old man pulled the skiff up onto him.

When he was even with him and had the fish's head against the bow he could not believe his size. But he untied the harpoon rope from the bitt, passed it through the fish's gills and out his jaws, made a turn around his sword then passed the rope through the other gill, made another turn around the bill and knotted the double rope and made it fast to the bitt in the bow. He cut the rope then and went astern to noose the tail. The fish had turned silver from his original purple and silver, and the stripes showed the same pale violet colour as his tail. They were wider than a man's hand with his fingers spread and the fish's eye looked as detached as the mirrors in a periscope or as a saint in a procession.

"It was the only way to kill him," the old man said. He was feeling better since the water and he knew he would not go away and his head was clear. He's over fifteen hundred pounds the way he is, he thought. Maybe much more. If he dresses out two-thirds of that at thirty cents a pound?

"I need a pencil for that," he said. "My head is not that clear. But I think the great DiMaggio would be proud of me today. I had no bone spurs. But the hands and the back hurt truly." I wonder what a bone spur is, he thought. Maybe we have them without knowing of it.

He made the fish fast to bow and stern and to the middle thwart. He was so big it was like lashing a much bigger skiff alongside. He cut a piece of line and tied the fish's lower jaw against his bill so his mouth would not open and they would sail as cleanly as possible. Then he stepped the mast and, with the stick that was his gaff and with his boom rigged, the patched sail drew, the boat began to move, and half lying in the stern he sailed south-west.

He did not need a compass to tell him where south-west was. He only needed the feel of the trade wind and the drawing of the sail. I better put a small line out with a spoon on it and try and get something to eat and drink for the moisture. But he could not find a spoon and his sardines were rotten. So he hooked a patch of yellow Gulf weed with the gaff as they passed and shook it so that the small shrimps that were in it fell onto the planking of the skiff. There were more than a dozen of them and they jumped and kicked like sand fleas. The old man pinched their heads off with his thumb and forefinger and ate them chewing up the shells and the tails. They were very tiny but he knew they were nourishing and they tasted good.

The old man still had two drinks of water in the bottle and he used half of one after he had eaten the shrimps. The skiff was sailing well considering the handicaps and he steered with the tiller under his arm. He could see the fish and he had only to look at his hands and feel his back against the stern to know that this had truly happened and was not a dream. At one time when he was feeling so badly toward the end, he had thought perhaps it was a dream. Then when he had seen the fish come out of the water and hang motionless in the sky before he fell, he was sure there was some great strangeness and he could not believe it. Then he could not see well, although now he saw as well as ever.

Now he knew there was the fish and his hands and back were no dream. The hands cure quickly, he thought. I bled them clean and the salt water will heal them. The dark water of the true gulf is the greatest healer that there is. All I must do is keep the head clear. The hands have done their work and we sail well. With his mouth shut and his tail straight up and down we sail like brothers. Then his head started to become a little unclear and he thought, is he bringing me in or am I bringing him in? If I were towing him behind there would be no question. Nor if the fish were in the skiff, with all dignity gone, there would be no question either. But they were sailing together lashed side by side and the old man thought, let him bring me in if it pleases him. I am only better than him through trickery and he meant me no harm.

They sailed well and the old man soaked his hands in the salt water and tried to keep his head clear. There were high cumulus clouds and enough cirrus above them so that the old man knew the breeze would last all night. The old man looked at the fish constantly to make sure it was true. It was an hour before the first shark hit him.

The shark was not an accident. He had come up from deep down in the water as the dark cloud of blood had settled and dispersed in the mile deep sea. He had come up so fast and absolutely without caution that he broke the surface of the blue water and was in the sun. Then he fell back into the sea and picked up the scent and started swimming on the course the skiff and the fish had taken.

Sometimes he lost the scent. But he would pick it up again, or have just a trace of it, and he swam fast and hard on the course. He was a very big Mako shark built to swim as fast as the fastest fish in the sea and everything about him was beautiful except his jaws. His back was as blue as a sword fish's and his belly was silver and his hide was smooth and handsome. He was built as a sword fish except for his huge jaws which were tight shut now as he swam fast, just under the surface with his high dorsal fin knifing through the water without wavering. Inside the closed double lip of his jaws all of his eight rows of teeth were slanted inwards. They were not the ordinary pyramid-shaped teeth of most sharks. They were shaped like a man's fingers when they are crisped like claws. They were nearly as long as the fingers of the old man and they had razor-sharp cutting edges on both sides. This was a fish built to feed on all the fishes in the sea, that were so fast and strong and well armed that they had no other enemy. Now he speeded up as he smelled the fresher scent and his blue dorsal fin cut the water.

When the old man saw him coming he knew that this was a shark that had no fear at all and would do exactly what he wished. He prepared the harpoon and made the rope fast while he watched the shark come on. The rope was short as it lacked what he had cut away to lash the fish.

The old man's head was clear and good now and he was full of resolution but he had little hope. It was too good to last, he thought. He took one look at the great fish as he watched the shark close in. It might as well have been a dream, he thought. I cannot keep him from hitting me but maybe I can get him. *Dentuso*, he thought. Bad luck to your mother.

The shark closed fast astern and when he hit the fish the old man saw his mouth open and his strange eyes and the clicking chop of the teeth as he drove forward in the meat just above the tail. The shark's head was out of water and his back was coming out and the old man could hear the noise of skin and flesh ripping on the big fish when he rammed the harpoon down onto the shark's head at a spot where the line between his eyes intersected with the line that ran straight back from his nose. There were no such lines. There was only the heavy sharp blue head and the big eyes and the clicking, thrusting all-swallowing jaws. But that was the location of the brain and the old man hit it. He hit it with his blood mushed hands driving a good harpoon with all his strength. He hit it without hope but with resolution and complete malignancy.

The shark swung over and the old man saw his eye was not alive and then he swung over once again, wrapping himself in two loops of the rope. The old man knew that he was dead but the shark would not accept it. Then, on his back, with his tail lashing and his jaws clicking, the shark plowed over the water as a speedboat does. The water was white where his tail beat it and three-quarters of his body was clear above the water when the rope came taut, shivered, and then snapped. The shark lay quietly for a little while on the surface and the old man watched him. Then he went down very slowly.

"He took about forty pounds," the old man said aloud. He took my harpoon too and all the rope, he thought, and now my fish bleeds again and there will be others.

He did not like to look at the fish anymore since he had

been mutilated. When the fish had been hit it was as though he himself were hit.

But I killed the shark that hit my fish, he thought. And he was the biggest *dentuso* that I have ever seen. And God knows that I have seen big ones.

It was too good to last, he thought. I wish it had been a dream now and that I had never hooked the fish and was alone in bed on the newspapers.

"But man is not made for defeat," he said. "A man can be destroyed but not defeated." I am sorry that I killed the fish though, he thought. Now the bad time is coming and I do not even have the harpoon. The *dentuso* is cruel and able and strong and intelligent. But I was more intelligent than he was. Perhaps not, he thought. Perhaps I was only better armed.

"Don't think, old man," he said aloud. "Sail on this course and take it when it comes."

But I must think, he thought. Because it is all I have left. That and baseball. I wonder how the great DiMaggio would have liked the way I hit him in the brain? It was no great thing, he thought. Any man could do it. But do you think my hands were as great a handicap as the bone spurs? I cannot know. I never had anything wrong with my heel except the time the sting ray stung it when I stepped on him when swimming and paralyzed the lower leg and made the unbearable pain.

"Think about something cheerful, old man," he said. "Every minute now you are closer to home. You sail lighter for the loss of forty pounds."

He knew quite well the pattern of what could happen when he reached the inner part of the current. But there was nothing to be done now.

"Yes there is," he said aloud. "I can lash my knife to the butt of one of the oars."

So he did that with the tiller under his arm and the sheet of the sail under his foot.

"Now," he said. "I am still an old man. But I am not unarmed."

The breeze was fresh now and he sailed on well. He watched only the forward part of the fish and some of his hope returned.

It is silly not to hope, he thought. Besides I believe it is a sin. Do not think about sin, he thought. There are enough problems now without sin. Also I have no understanding of it.

I have no understanding of it and I am not sure that I believe in it. Perhaps it was a sin to kill the fish. I suppose it was even though I did it to keep me alive and feed many people. But then everything is a sin. Do not think about sin. It is much too late for that and there are people who are paid to do it. Let them think about it. You were born to be a fisherman as the fish was born to be a fish. San Pedro was a fisherman as was the father of the great DiMaggio.

But he liked to think about all things that he was involved in and since there was nothing to read and he did not have a radio, he thought much and he kept on thinking about sin. You did not kill the fish only to keep alive and to sell for food, he thought. You killed him for pride and because you are a fisherman. You loved him when he was alive and you loved him after. If you love him, it is not a sin to kill him. Or is it more?

"You think too much, old man," he said aloud.

But you enjoyed killing the *dentuso*, he thought. He

lives on the live fish as you do. He is not a scavenger nor just a moving appetite as some sharks are. He is beautiful and noble and knows no fear of anything.

"I killed him in self-defense," the old man said aloud. "And I killed him well."

Besides, he thought, everything kills everything else in some way. Fishing kills me exactly as it keeps me alive. The boy keeps me alive, he thought. I must not deceive myself too much.

He leaned over the side and pulled loose a piece of the meat of the fish where the shark had cut him. He chewed it and noted its quality and its good taste. It was firm and juicy, like meat, but it was not red. There was no stringiness in it and he knew that it would bring the highest price in the market. But there was no way to keep its scent out of the water and the old man knew that a very bad time was coming.

The breeze was steady. It had backed a little further into the north-east and he knew that meant that it would not fall off. The old man looked ahead of him but he could see no sails nor could he see the hull nor the smoke of any ship. There were only the flying fish that went up from his bow sailing away to either side and the yellow patches of Gulf weed. He could not even see a bird.

He had sailed for two hours, resting in the stern and sometimes chewing a bit of the meat from the marlin, trying to rest and to be strong, when he saw the first of the two sharks.

"*Ay,*" he said aloud. There is no translation for this word and perhaps it is just a noise such as a man might make, involuntarily, feeling the nail go through his hands and into the wood.

"*Galanos*," he said aloud. He had seen the second fin now coming up behind the first and had identified them as shovel-nosed sharks by the brown, triangular fin and the sweeping movements of the tail. They had the scent and were excited and in the stupidity of their great hunger they were losing and finding the scent in their excitement. But they were closing all the time.

The old man made the sheet fast and jammed the tiller. Then he took up the oar with the knife lashed to it. He lifted it as lightly as he could because his hands rebelled at the pain. Then he opened and closed them on it lightly to loosen them. He closed them firmly so they would take the pain now and would not flinch and watched the sharks come. He could see their wide, flattened, shovel-pointed heads now and their white-tipped wide pectoral fins. They were hateful sharks, bad smelling, scavengers as well as killers, and when they were hungry they would bite at an oar or the rudder of a boat. It was these sharks that would cut the turtles' legs and flippers off when the turtles were asleep on the surface, and they would hit a man in the water, if they were hungry, even if the man had no smell of fish blood nor of fish slime on him.

"*Ay*," the old man said. "*Galanos*. Come on *galanos*."

They came. But they did not come as the Mako had come. One turned and went out of sight under the skiff and the old man could feel the skiff shake as he jerked and pulled on the fish. The other watched the old man with his slitted yellow eyes and then came in fast with his half circle of jaws wide to hit the fish where he had already been bitten. The line showed clearly on the top of his brown head and back where the brain joined the spinal cord and the old man drove the knife on the oar into the juncture, withdrew it, and drove it in again into the shark's yellow cat-like eyes. The shark let go of the fish and slid down, swallowing what he had taken as he died.

The skiff was still shaking with the destruction the other shark was doing to the fish and the old man let go the sheet so that the skiff would swing broadside and bring the shark out from under. When he saw the shark he leaned over the side and punched at him. He hit only meat and the hide was set hard and he barely got the knife in. The blow hurt not only his hands but his shoulder too. But the shark came up fast with his head out and the old man hit him squarely in the center of his flat-topped head as his nose came out of water and lay against the fish. The old man withdrew the blade and punched the shark exactly in the same spot again. He still hung to the fish with his jaws hooked and the old man stabbed him in his left eye. The shark still hung there.

"No?" the old man said and he drove the blade between the vertebrae and the brain. It was an easy shot now and he felt the cartilage sever. The old man reversed the oar and put the blade between the shark's jaws to open them. He twisted the blade and as the shark slid loose he said, "Go on, *galano*. Slide down a mile deep. Go see your friend, or maybe it's your mother."

The old man wiped the blade of his knife and laid down the oar. Then he found the sheet and the sail filled and he brought the skiff onto her course.

"They must have taken a quarter of him and of the best meat," he said aloud. "I wish it were a dream and that I had never hooked him. I'm sorry about it, fish. It makes everything wrong." He stopped and he did not want to look at the fish now. Drained of blood and awash he looked the colour of the silver backing of a mirror and his stripes still showed.

"I shouldn't have gone out so far, fish," he said. "Neither for you nor for me. I'm sorry, fish."

Now, he said to himself. Look to the lashing on the knife and see if it has been cut. Then get your hand in order because there still is more to come.

"I wish I had a stone for the knife," the old man said after he had checked the lashing on the oar butt. "I should have brought a stone." You should have brought many things, he thought. But you did not bring them, old man. Now is no time to think of what you do not have. Think of what you can do with what there is.

"You give me much good counsel," he said aloud. "I'm tired of it."

He held the tiller under his arm and soaked both his hands in the water as the skiff drove forward.

"God knows how much that last one took," he said. "But she's much lighter now." He did not want to think of the mutilated under-side of the fish. He knew that each of the jerking bumps of the shark had been meat torn away and that the fish now made a trail for all sharks as wide as a highway through the sea.

He was a fish to keep a man all winter, he thought. Don't think of that. Just rest and try to get your hands in shape to defend what is left of him. The blood smell from my hands means nothing now with all that scent in the water. Besides they do not bleed much. There is nothing cut that means anything. The bleeding may keep the left from cramping.

What can I think of now? he thought. Nothing. I must think of nothing and wait for the next ones. I wish it had really been a dream, he thought. But who knows? It might have turned out well.

The next shark that came was a single shovelnose. He came like a pig to the trough if a pig had a mouth so wide that you could put your head in it. The old man let him hit the fish and then drove the knife on the oar down into his brain. But the shark jerked backwards as he rolled and the knife blade snapped.

The old man settled himself to steer. He did not even watch the big shark sinking slowly in the water, showing first life-size, then small, then tiny. That always fascinated the old man. But he did not even watch it now.

"I have the gaff now," he said. "But it will do no good. I have the two oars and the tiller and the short club."

Now they have beaten me, he thought. I am too old to club sharks to death. But I will try it as long as I have the oars and the short club and the tiller.

He put his hands in the water again to soak them. It was getting late in the afternoon and he saw nothing but the sea and the sky. There was more wind in the sky than there had been, and soon he hoped that he would see land.

"You're tired, old man," he said. "You're tired inside."

The sharks did not hit him again until just before sunset.

The old man saw the brown fins coming along the wide trail the fish must make in the water. They were not even quartering on the scent. They were headed straight for the skiff swimming side by side.

He jammed the tiller, made the sheet fast and reached under the stern for the club. It was an oar handle from a broken oar sawed off to about two and a half feet in length. He could only use it effectively with one hand because of the grip of the handle and he took good hold of it with his right hand, flexing his hand on it, as he watched the sharks come. They were both *galanos*.

I must let the first one get a good hold and hit him on the point of the nose or straight across the top of the head, he thought.

The two sharks closed together and as he saw the one nearest him open his jaws and sink them into the silver side of the fish, he raised the club high and brought it down heavy and slamming onto the top of the shark's broad head. He felt the rubbery solidity as the club came down. But he felt the rigidity of bone too and he struck the shark once more hard across the point of the nose as he slid down from the fish.

The other shark had been in and out and now came in again with his jaws wide. The old man could see pieces of the meat of the fish spilling white from the corner of his jaws as he bumped the fish and closed his jaws. He swung at him and hit only the head and the shark looked at him and wrenched the meat loose. The old man swung the club down on him again as he slipped away to swallow and hit only the heavy solid rubberiness.

"Come on, *galano*," the old man said. "Come in again."

The shark came in a rush and the old man hit him as he shut his jaws. He hit him solidly and from as high up as he could raise the club. This time he felt the bone at the base of the brain and he hit him again in the same place while the shark tore the meat loose sluggishly and slid down from the fish.

The old man watched for him to come again but neither shark showed. Then he saw one on the surface swimming in circles. He did not see the fin of the other.

I could not expect to kill them, he thought. I could

have in my time. But I have hurt them both badly and neither one can feel very good. If I could have used a bat with two hands I could have killed the first one surely. Even now, he thought.

He did not want to look at the fish. He knew that half of him had been destroyed. The sun had gone down while he had been in the fight with the sharks.

"It will be dark soon," he said. "Then I should see the glow of Havana. If I am too far to the eastward I will see the lights of one of the new beaches."

I cannot be too far out now, he thought. I hope no one has been too worried. There is only the boy to worry, of course. But I am sure he would have confidence. Many of the older fishermen will worry. Many others too, he thought. I live in a good town.

He could not talk to the fish anymore because the fish had been ruined too badly. Then something came into his head.

"Half fish," he said. "Fish that you were. I am sorry that I went too far out. I ruined us both. But we have killed many sharks, you and I, and ruined many others. How many did you ever kill, old fish? You do not have that spear on your head for nothing."

He liked to think of the fish and what he could do to a shark if he were swimming free. I should have chopped the bill off to fight them with, he thought. But there was no hatchet and then there was no knife.

But if I had, and could have lashed it to an oar butt, what a weapon. Then we might have fought them together. What will you do now if they come in the night? What can you do?

"Fight them," he said. "I'll fight them until I die."

Figure 1. Ernest Hemingway, Carlos Gutiérrez, Joe Russell, and Joe Lowe aboard the *Anita* with a marlin, 1933. Ernest Hemingway Collection, John F. Kennedy Presidential Library and Museum, Boston, MA.

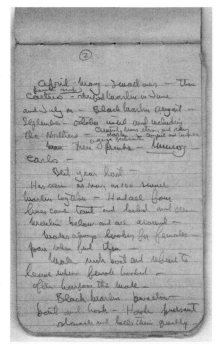

Figure 2. Ernest Hemingway's fishing log from 1932. Page with notes from talks with Carlos Gutiérrez about marlin fishing. Ernest Hemingway Collection, Oversize Materials, Box 14, Folder 13, page 9, at the John F. Kennedy Presidential Library and Museum, Boston, MA.

Figure 3. Ernest Hemingway and Carlos Gutiérrez at the wheel of the *Pilar*, 1934. Ernest Hemingway Collection, John F. Kennedy Presidential Library and Museum, Boston, MA.

Figure 4. Hemingway's fishing cruiser, the *Pilar*. Hemingway is standing on the dock immediately to the left of the marlin, circa 1934. Ernest Hemingway Collection, John F. Kennedy Presidential Library and Museum, Boston, MA.

Figure 5. The *Pilar* under way. Note the outriggers, which were added in April 1935. Ernest Hemingway Collection, John F. Kennedy Presidential Library and Museum, Boston, MA.

Figure 6. Pauline Hemingway, Ernest Hemingway, and his three sons, Jack, Patrick, and Gregory, with four blue marlin, Brown's Dock, Bimini, July 1935. Ernest Hemingway Collection, John F. Kennedy Presidential Library and Museum, Boston, MA.

Figure 7. Cuban fishing skiff. Photo by Ernest Hemingway. Ernest Hemingway Collection, John F. Kennedy Presidential Library and Museum, Boston, MA.

Figure 8. Cuban fishermen landing a shark. Ernest Hemingway Collection, John F. Kennedy Presidential Library and Museum, Boston, MA.

Figure 9. Fishermen from Cojímar, Cuba, bringing back a marlin, 1955. Photo attributed to Ernest Hemingway. Ernest Hemingway Collection, John F. Kennedy Presidential Library and Museum, Boston, MA.

Principal Sharks in Cuban Waters

Local Name English Name Remarks

Dentuso Mako Shark Rare .Vicious .Grows to 1000 pounds and over . Could be man-eater but ordinarily follows schools of mackerel and swordfish .

Cornuda Hammerhead - Common ,especially in spring and summer . Frequents entrances of harbours and small rivers and along reefs . Is definitely a maneating shark and reaches weights of 1200 and over . Rarely attacks during breeding period in April .

Cabeza Batea Tiger Shark - Abundant ,slow , stupid shark which will eat anything from garbage to gasoline tins . When blood is present in water, will attack anything including men . Reaches 1000 pounds but most common at 400-600 pounds. They have been known to take bathers from the rocky beaches off the Punta Brava at Havana and if they have become man eaters are dangerous .

Galano Shovel Nose - Most common cuban shark and the most consistently dangerous . If hungry they will attack anything . If not hungry they are shy and wary . They are found in all parts of the gulf stream and will come instantly to the scent of blood . Have a fine sense of smell - will come where any objects dropped in water especially those containing grease or anything nauseous . The smell of blood maddens them so that they will attack blindly even when wounded .

Tiburon de Ley - White Shark or True Shark - Comparatively rare . Have never known them to be maneaters as they are comparatively shy and never attack hooked fish . They are found only in the gulf stream . Very powerful shark . Reach great weight . Much nonsense has been written about this shark as a maneater . Off Cuban coast those shark which have attacked human beings have been the Hammerhead ,Galano , or Tiger shark . The Mako will rush at a man who has him hooked but he is primarily a fish-eating shark and there are no instances of his ever having attacked human beings as far as I know .

Boca Dulce - BluesFin or SoupsFin shark — An exceedingly shy fish-eating shark which is only caught at night . No instances of ever attacking human beings .

Gata Nurse Shark- Abundant in shallows . Has no teeth . Dark brown in colour . Absolutely inoffensive .

Zorro Threaher Shark - Very shy shark in deep water . Never attacks human beings, nor hooked fish .

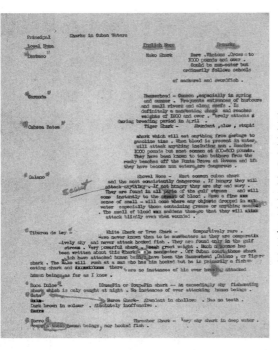

Figure 10. Ernest Hemingway's List of Principle Sharks in Cuban Waters. Ernest Hemingway Collection, Manuscripts Series, Box 57, Folder 10, page 1, at the John F. Kennedy Presidential Library and Museum, Boston, MA.

That year we had planned to fish for marlin off the Cuban coast for a month . The month started the tenth of April and by the the tenth of May we had twenty five marlin and the charter was over . The thing to have done then would have been to buy some presents to take back to Key West , fill the" Anita " with just a little more than the expensive Cuban gas necessary to run across , get cleared and go home . But the big fish had not started to run .

" Do you want to try her another month ,Cap ?" Mr. Josie asked . He owned the Anita and was chartering her for ten dollars a day . The standard charter price then was thirty five a day . " If you want to stay I can cut her to nine dollars a day ."

" Where would we get the nine dollars ?"

" You pay me when you get it . You got good credit with the Standard Oil Company at Belot across the bay and I can pay them when we get the bill from last month's charter money . If we get bad weather you can write something ."

" All right ," I said and we fished another month . We had forty two marling by then and still the big ones had not come . There was a dark ,heavy stream close in to the Morro ,acres of bait ,and birds working all the time . But we had not raised one of the huge marlin . But we were catching ,or losing , white marlin each day and on one day I caught five .

We were very popular along the water front because we butchered all our fish and gave them away and when we would come up the channel toward the San Francisco docks with a marlin flag up you could see the crowd starting to run for the docks . The fish was worth from eight to twelve cents a pound that year to a fisherman and twice that in the market .The day we came in with five flags the police had to charge the crowd with clubs . It was ugly and bad .But that was an ugly and bad year ashore .

" The goddam police running off our regular clients and getting all the fish ," Mr. Josie said . "To hell with you ," he told

Figure 11. First manuscript page of the short story "Pursuit As Happiness." Ernest Hemingway Collection, Manuscripts Series, Box 59, Folder 19, page 1, at the John F. Kennedy Presidential Library and Museum, Boston, MA.

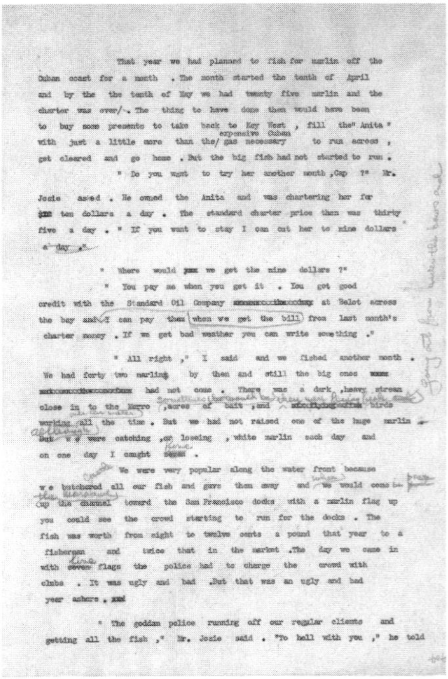

E's Typescript -

He was an old man who fished alone in a skiff in the Gulf Stream and he had gone eighty four days now without taking a fish . In the first forty days a boy had been with him .But after forty days without a fish the boy's parents had told him that the old man was now definitely and finally salao , which is the worst form of unlucky , and the boy had gone at their orders in another boat which caught three good fish the first week . It made the boy sad to see the old man come in each day with his skiff empty and he always went down to help him carry either the coiled lines or the gaff and harpoon and the sail that was furled around the mast . The sail was patched with flour sacks and , furled , it looked like the flag of permanent defeat .

The old man was thin and gaunt with deep wrinkles in the back of his neck .The brown blotches of the benevolent skin cancer the sun brings from its reflection on the tropic sea were on his cheeks .The blotches ran well down the sides of his face and his hands had the deep -creased scars from handling heavy fish on the cords . But none of these scars were fresh . They were as old as erosions in a fishless desert .

Everything about him was old except his eyes and they were the same color as the sea and were cheerful and undefeated .

"Santiago ," the boy said to him as they climbed the bank from where the skiff was hauled up ." I could go with you again . We've made some money . "

The old man had taught the boy to fish and the boy loved him .

"No," the old man said . "You're with a lucky boat . Stay with them ."

"But remember how you went eighty seven days without fish

Figure 12. First page of Hemingway's typescript of *The Old Man and the Sea*. Ernest Hemingway Collection, Item 90, Manuscripts Series, Box 27, Folder 5, page 1, at the John F. Kennedy Presidential Library and Museum, Boston, MA.

96

What can I think of now ? he thought . Nothing . I must think of nothing and wait for the next ones . I wish it had really been a dream ,he thought . But who knows ? It might have turned out well .

The next shark that came was a single shovel nose . He came like a pig to the trough if a pig had a mouth so wide that you could put your head in it .The old man let him hit the fish and then drove the knife on the oar down into his brain . But the shark jerked backwards as he rolled and the knife blade snapped .

The old man settled himself to steer . He did not even watch the big shark sinking slowly in the water

"I have the gaff now ," he said . "But it will do no good . I have the two oars and the tiller and the short club ."

Now they have beaten me , he thought . I am too old to club sharks to death . But I will try it as long as I have the oars and the short club and the tiller .

He put his hands in the water again to soak them . It was getting late in the afternoon and he saw nothing but the sea and the sky . There was more wind in the sky than there had been and soon he hoped that he would see land .

"You're tired ,old man ," he said . "You're

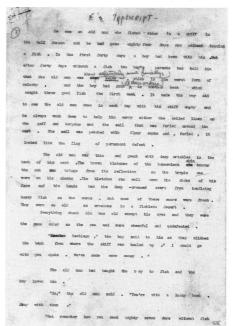

Figure 13. Page 96 of Hemingway's typescript of *The Old Man and the Sea*. Ernest Hemingway Collection, Item 90, Manuscripts Series, Box 27, Folder 8, page 96, at the John F. Kennedy Presidential Library and Museum, Boston, MA.

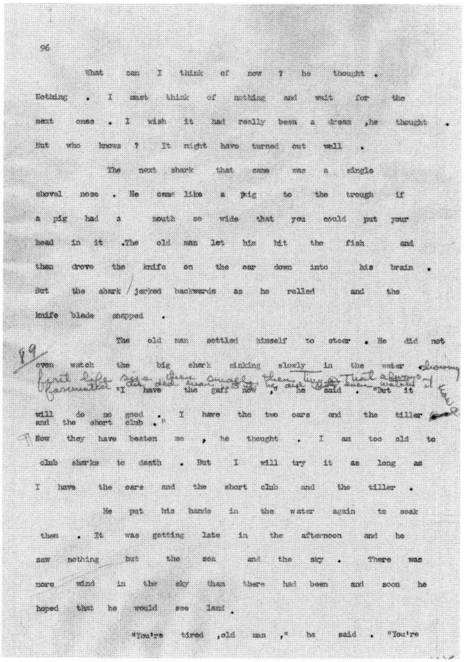

Figure 14. Cover of *Life* magazine, September 1, 1952, issue, featuring *The Old Man and the Sea*. Ernest Hemingway Collection, John F. Kennedy Presidential Library and Museum, Boston, MA.

Figure 15. The original dust jacket cover of *The Old Man and the Sea*, 1952.

But in the dark now and no glow showing and no lights and only the wind and the steady pull of the sail he felt that perhaps he was already dead. He put his two hands together and felt the palms. They were not dead and he could bring the pain of life by simply opening and closing them. He leaned his back against the stern and knew he was not dead. His shoulders told him.

I have all those prayers I promised if I caught the fish, he thought. But I am too tired to say them now. I better get the sack and put it over my shoulders.

He lay in the stern and steered and watched for the glow to come in the sky. I have half of him, he thought. Maybe I'll have the luck to bring the forward half in. I should have some luck. No, he said. You violated your luck when you went too far outside.

"Don't be silly," he said aloud. "And keep awake and steer. You may have much luck yet."

"I'd like to buy some if there's any place they sell it," he said.

What could I buy it with? he asked himself. Could I buy it with a lost harpoon and a broken knife and two bad hands?

"You might," he said. "You tried to buy it with eighty-four days at sea. They nearly sold it to you too."

I must not think nonsense, he thought. Luck is a thing that comes in many forms and who can recognize her? I would take some though in any form and pay what they asked. I wish I could see the glow from the lights, he thought. I wish too many things. But that is the thing I wish for now. He tried to settle more comfortably to steer and from his pain he knew he was not dead.

He saw the reflected glare of the lights of the city at

what must have been around ten o'clock at night. They were only perceptible at first as the light is in the sky before the moon rises. Then they were steady to see across the ocean which was rough now with the increasing breeze. He steered inside of the glow and he thought that now, soon, he must hit the edge of the stream.

Now it is over, he thought. They will probably hit me again. But what can a man do against them in the dark without a weapon?

He was stiff and sore now and his wounds and all of the strained parts of his body hurt with the cold of the night. I hope I do not have to fight again, he thought. I hope so much I do not have to fight again.

But by midnight he fought and this time he knew the fight was useless. They came in a pack and he could only see the lines in the water that their fins made and their phosphorescence as they threw themselves on the fish. He clubbed at heads and heard the jaws chop and the shaking of the skiff as they took hold below. He clubbed desperately at what he could only feel and hear and he felt something seize the club and it was gone.

He jerked the tiller free from the rudder and beat and chopped with it, holding it in both hands and driving it down again and again. But they were up to the bow now and driving in one after the other and together, tearing off the pieces of meat that showed glowing below the sea as they turned to come once more.

One came, finally, against the head itself and he knew that it was over. He swung the tiller across the shark's head where the jaws were caught in the heaviness of the fish's head which would not tear. He swung it once and twice and again. He heard the tiller break and he lunged at the shark with the splintered butt. He felt it go in and knowing it was sharp he drove it in again. The shark let go and rolled away. That was the last shark of the pack that came. There was nothing more for them to eat.

The old man could hardly breathe now and he felt a strange taste in his mouth. It was coppery and sweet and he was afraid of it for a moment. But there was not much of it.

He spat into the ocean and said, "Eat that, *galanos*. And make a dream you've killed a man."

He knew he was beaten now finally and without remedy and he went back to the stern and found the jagged end of the tiller would fit in the slot of the rudder well enough for him to steer. He settled the sack around his shoulders and put the skiff on her course. He sailed lightly now and he had no thoughts nor any feelings of any kind. He was past everything now and he sailed the skiff to make his home port as well and as intelligently as he could. In the night sharks hit the carcass as someone might pick up crumbs from the table. The old man paid no attention to them and did not pay any attention to anything except steering. He only noticed how lightly and how well the skiff sailed now there was no great weight beside her.

She's good, he thought. She is sound and not harmed in any way except for the tiller. That is easily replaced.

He could feel he was inside the current now and he could see the lights of the beach colonies along the shore. He knew where he was now and it was nothing to get home.

The wind is our friend, anyway, he thought. Then he added, sometimes. And the great sea with our friends and our enemies. And bed, he thought. Bed is my friend. Just bed, he thought. Bed will be a great thing. It is easy when you are beaten, he thought. I never knew how easy it was. And what beat you, he thought.

"Nothing," he said aloud. "I went out too far."

When he sailed into the little harbour the lights of the Terrace were out and he knew everyone was in bed. The breeze had risen steadily and was blowing strongly now. It was quiet in the harbour though and he sailed up onto the little patch of shingle below the rocks. There was no one to help him so he pulled the boat up as far as he could. Then he stepped out and made her fast to a rock.

He unstepped the mast and furled the sail and tied it. Then he shouldered the mast and started to climb. It was then he knew the depth of his tiredness. He stopped for a moment and looked back and saw in the reflection from the street light the great tail of the fish standing up well behind the skiff's stern. He saw the white naked line of his backbone and the dark mass of the head with the projecting bill and all the nakedness between.

He started to climb again and at the top he fell and lay for some time with the mast across his shoulder. He tried to get up. But it was too difficult and he sat there with the mast on his shoulder and looked at the road. A cat passed on the far side going about its business and the old man watched it. Then he just watched the road.

Finally he put the mast down and stood up. He picked the mast up and put it on his shoulder and started up the road. He had to sit down five times before he reached his shack.

Inside the shack he leaned the mast against the wall. In the dark he found a water bottle and took a drink. Then he lay down on the bed. He pulled the blanket over his shoulders and then over his back and legs and he slept face down on the newspapers with his arms out straight and the palms of his hands up.

He was asleep when the boy looked in the door in the morning. It was blowing so hard that the drifting boats would not be going out and the boy had slept late and then come to the old man's shack as he had come each morning. The boy saw that the old man was breathing and then he saw the old man's hands and he started to cry. He went out very quietly to go to bring some coffee and all the way down the road he was crying.

Many fishermen were around the skiff looking at what was lashed beside it and one was in the water, his trousers rolled up, measuring the skeleton with a length of line.

The boy did not go down. He had been there before and one of the fishermen was looking after the skiff for him.

"How is he?" one of the fishermen shouted.

"Sleeping," the boy called. He did not care that they saw him crying. "Let no one disturb him."

"He was eighteen feet from nose to tail," the fisherman who was measuring him called.

"I believe it," the boy said.

He went into the Terrace and asked for a can of coffee.

"Hot and with plenty of milk and sugar in it."

"Anything more?"

"No. Afterwards I will see what he can eat."

"What a fish it was," the proprietor said. "There has never been such a fish. Those were two fine fish you took yesterday too."

"Damn my fish," the boy said and he started to cry again.

"Do you want a drink of any kind?" the proprietor asked.

"No," the boy said. "Tell them not to bother Santiago. I'll be back."

"Tell him how sorry I am."

"Thanks," the boy said.

The boy carried the hot can of coffee up to the old man's shack and sat by him until he woke. Once it looked as though he were waking. But he had gone back into heavy sleep and the boy had gone across the road to borrow some wood to heat the coffee.

Finally the old man woke.

"Don't sit up," the boy said. "Drink this." He poured some of the coffee in a glass.

The old man took it and drank it.

"They beat me, Manolin," he said. "They truly beat me."

"*He* didn't beat you. Not the fish."

"No. Truly. It was afterwards."

"Pedrico is looking after the skiff and the gear. What do you want done with the head?"

"Let Pedrico chop it up to use in fish traps."

"And the spear?"

"You keep it if you want it."

"I want it," the boy said. "Now we must make our plans about the other things."

"Did they search for me?"

"Of course. With coast guard and with planes."

"The ocean is very big and a skiff is small and hard to see," the old man said. He noticed how pleasant it was to have someone to talk to instead of speaking only to himself and to the sea. "I missed you," he said. "What did you catch?"

"One the first day. One the second and two the third."

"Very good."

"Now we fish together again."

"No. I am not lucky. I am not lucky anymore."

"The hell with luck," the boy said. "I'll bring the luck with me."

"What will your family say?"

"I do not care. I caught two yesterday. But we will fish together now for I still have much to learn."

"We must get a good killing lance and always have it on board. You can make the blade from a spring leaf from an old Ford. We can grind it in Guanabacoa. It should be sharp and not tempered so it will break. My knife broke."

"I'll get another knife and have the spring ground. How many days of heavy *brisa* have we?"

"Maybe three. Maybe more."

"I will have everything in order," the boy said. "You get your hands well old man."

"I know how to care for them. In the night I spat something strange and felt something in my chest was broken."

"Get that well too," the boy said. "Lie down, old man, and I will bring you your clean shirt. And something to eat."

"Bring any of the papers of the time that I was gone," the old man said.

"You must get well fast for there is much that I can learn and you can teach me everything. How much did you suffer?"

"Plenty," the old man said.

"I'll bring the food and the papers," the boy said. "Rest well, old man. I will bring stuff from the drugstore for your hands."

"Don't forget to tell Pedrico the head is his."

"No. I will remember."

As the boy went out the door and down the worn coral rock road he was crying again.

That afternoon there was a party of tourists at the Terrace and looking down in the water among the empty beer cans and dead barracudas a woman saw a great long white spine with a huge tail at the end that lifted and swung with the tide while the east wind blew a heavy steady sea outside the entrance to the harbour.

"What's that?" she asked a waiter and pointed to the long backbone of the great fish that was now just garbage waiting to go out with the tide.

"Tiburon," the waiter said. "Eshark." He was meaning to explain what had happened.

"I didn't know sharks had such handsome, beautifully formed tails."

"I didn't either," her male companion said.

Up the road, in his shack, the old man was sleeping again. He was still sleeping on his face and the boy was sitting by him watching him. The old man was dreaming about the lions.

Appendix I

"On the Blue Water: A Gulf Stream Letter" First published in *Esquire*, April 1936

Certainly there is no hunting like the hunting of man and those who have hunted armed men long enough and liked it, never really care for anything else thereafter. You will meet them doing various things with resolve, but their interest rarely holds because after the other thing ordinary life is as flat as the taste of wine when the taste buds have been burned off your tongue. Wine, when your tongue has been burned clean with lye and water, feels like puddle water in your mouth, while mustard feels like axle-grease, and you can smell crisp, fried bacon, but when you taste it, there is only a feeling of crinkly lard.

You can learn about this matter of the tongue by coming into the kitchen of a villa on the Riviera late at night and taking a drink from what should be a bottle of Evian water and which turns out to be *Eau de Javel*, a concentrated lye product used for cleaning sinks. The taste buds on your tongue, if burned off by *Eau de Javel*, will begin to function again after about a week. At what rate other things regenerate one does not know, since you lose track of friends and the things one could learn in a week were mostly learned a long time ago.

The other night I was talking with a good friend to whom all hunting is dull except elephant hunting. To him there is no sport in anything unless there is great danger and, if the danger is not enough, he will increase it for his own satisfaction. A hunting companion of his had told me how this friend was not satisfied with the risks of ordinary elephant hunting but would, if possible, have the elephants driven, or turned, so he could take them head-on, so it was a choice of killing them with the difficult frontal shot as they came, trumpeting, with their ears spread, or having them run over him. This is to elephant hunting what the German cult of suicide climbing is to ordinary mountaineering, and I suppose it is, in a way, an attempt to approximate the old hunting of the armed man who is hunting you.

This friend was speaking of elephant hunting and urging me to hunt elephant, as he said that once you took it up no other hunting would mean anything to you. I was arguing that I enjoyed all hunting and shooting, any sort I could get, and had no desire to wipe this capacity for enjoyment out with the *Eau de Javel* of the old elephant coming straight at you with his trunk up and his ears spread.

"Of course you like that big fishing too," he said rather sadly. "Frankly, I can't see where the excitement is in that."

"You'd think it was marvelous if the fish shot at you with Tommy guns or jumped back and forth through the cockpit with swords on the ends of their noses."

"Don't be silly," he said. "But frankly I don't see where the thrill is."

"Look at so and so," I said. "He's an elephant hunter and this last year he's gone fishing for big fish and he's goofy about it. He must get a kick out of it or he wouldn't do it."

"Yes," my friend said. "There must be something about it but I can't see it. Tell me where you get a thrill out of it."

"I'll try to write it in a piece sometime," I told him.

"I wish you would," he said. "Because you people are sensible on other subjects. Moderately sensible I mean."

"I'll write it."

In the first place, the Gulf Stream and the other great ocean currents are the last wild country there is left. Once you are out of sight of land and of the other boats you are more alone than you can ever be hunting and the sea is the same as it has been since before men ever went on it in boats. In a season fishing you will see it oily flat as the becalmed galleons saw it while they drifted to the westward; white-capped with a fresh breeze as they saw it running with the trades; and in high, rolling blue hills the tops blowing off them like snow as they were punished by it, so that sometimes you will see three great hills of water with your fish jumping from the top of the farthest one and if you tried to make a turn to go with him without picking your chance, one of those breaking crests would roar down in on you with a thousand tons of water and you would hunt no more elephants, Richard, my lad.

There is no danger from the fish, but anyone who goes on the sea the year around in a small power boat does not seek danger. You may be absolutely sure that in a year you will have it without seeking, so you try always to avoid it all you can.

Because the Gulf Stream is an unexploited country, only the very fringe of it ever being fished, and then only at a dozen places in thousands of miles of current, no one knows what fish live in it, or how great size they reach or what age, or even what kinds of fish and animals live in it at different depths. When you are drifting, out of sight of land, fishing four lines, sixty, eighty, one hundred and one hundred fifty fathoms down, in water that is seven hundred fathoms deep you never know what may take the small tuna that you use for bait, and every time the line starts to run off the reel, slowly first, then with a scream of the click as the rod bends and you feel it double and the huge weight of the friction of the line rushing through that depth of water while you pump and reel, pump and reel, pump and reel, trying to get the belly out of the line before the fish jumps, there is always a thrill that needs no danger to make it real. It may be a marlin that will jump high and clear off to your right and then go off in a series of leaps, throwing a splash like a speedboat in a sea as you shout for the boat to turn with him watching the line melting off the reel before the boat can get around. Or it may be a broadbill that will show wagging his great broadsword. Or it may be some fish that you will never see at all that will head straight out to the northwest like a submerged submarine and never show and at the end of five hours the angler has a straightened-out hook. There is always a feeling of excitement when a fish takes hold when you are drifting deep.

In hunting you know what you are after and the top you can get is an elephant. But who can say what you will hook sometime when drifting in a hundred and fifty fathoms in the Gulf Stream? There are probably marlin and swordfish to which the fish we have seen caught are pygmies; and every time a fish takes the bait drifting you have a feeling perhaps you are hooked to one of these.

Carlos, our Cuban mate, who is fifty-three years old

and has been fishing for marlin since he went in the bow of a skiff with his father when he was seven, was fishing drifting deep one time when he hooked a white marlin. The fish jumped twice and then sounded and when he sounded suddenly Carlos felt a great weight and he could not hold the line which went out and down and down irresistibly until the fish had taken out over a hundred and fifty fathoms. Carlos says it felt as heavy and solid as though he were hooked to the bottom of the sea. Then suddenly the strain was loosened but he could feel the weight of his original fish and pulled it up stone dead. Some toothless fish like a swordfish or marlin had closed his jaws across the middle of the eighty-pound white marlin and squeezed it and held it so that every bit of the insides of the fish had been crushed out while the huge fish moved off with the eighty-pound fish in its mouth. Finally it let go. What size of a fish would that be? I thought it might be a giant squid but Carlos said there were no sucker marks on the fish and that it showed plainly the shape of the marlin's mouth where he had crushed it.

Another time an old man fishing alone in a skiff out of Cabañas hooked a great marlin that, on the heavy sash-cord handline, pulled the skiff far out to sea. Two days later the old man was picked up by fishermen sixty miles to the eastward, the head and forward part of the marlin lashed alongside. What was left of the fish, less than half, weighed eight hundred pounds. The old man had stayed with him a day, a night, a day and another night while the fish swam deep and pulled the boat. When he had come up the old man had pulled the boat up on him and harpooned him. Lashed alongside the sharks had hit him and the old man had fought them out alone in the Gulf Stream in a skiff, clubbing them, stabbing at them, lunging at them with an oar until he was exhausted and the sharks had eaten all that they could hold. He was crying in the boat when the fishermen picked him up, half crazy from his loss, and the sharks were still circling the boat.

But what is the excitement in catching them from a launch? It comes from the fact that they are strange and wild things of unbelievable speed and power and a beauty, in the water and leaping, that is indescribable, which you would never see if you did not fish for them, and to which you are suddenly harnessed so that you feel their speed, their force and their savage power as intimately as if you were riding a bucking horse. For half an hour, an hour, or five hours, you are fastened to the fish as much as he is fastened to you and you tame him and break him the way a wild horse is broken and finally lead him to the boat. For pride and because the fish is worth plenty of money in the Havana market, you gaff him at the boat and bring him on board, but the having him in the boat isn't the excitement; it is while you are fighting him that is the fun.

If the fish is hooked in the bony part of the mouth I am sure the hook hurts him no more than the harness hurts the angler. A large fish when he is hooked often does not feel the hook at all and will swim toward the boat, unconcerned, to take another bait. At other times he will swim away deep, completely unconscious of the hook, and it is when he feels himself held and pressure exerted to turn him, that he knows something is wrong and starts to make his fight. Unless he is hooked where it hurts he makes his fight not against the pain of the hook, but against being captured and if, when he is out of sight, you figure what he is doing, in what direction he is pulling when deep down, and why, you can convince him and bring him to the boat by the same system you break a wild horse. It is not necessary to kill him, or even completely exhaust him to bring him to the boat.

To kill a fish that fights deep you pull against the direction he wants to go until he is worn out and dies. It takes hours and when the fish dies the sharks are liable to get him before the angler can raise him to the top. To catch such a fish quickly you figure by trying to hold him absolutely, which direction he is working (a sounding fish is going in the direction the line slants in the water when you have put enough pressure on the drag so the line would break if you held it any tighter); then get ahead of him on that direction and he can be brought to the boat without killing him. You do not tow him or pull him with the motor boat; you use the engine to shift your position just as you would walk up or down stream with a salmon. A fish is caught most surely from a small boat such as a dory since the angler can shut down on his drag and simply let the fish pull the boat. Towing the boat will kill him in time. But the most satisfaction is to dominate and convince the fish and bring him intact in everything but spirit to the boat as rapidly as possible.

"Very instructive," says the friend. "But where does the thrill come in?"

The thrill comes when you are standing at the wheel drinking a cold bottle of beer and watching the outriggers jump the baits so they look like small live tuna leaping along and then behind one you see a long dark shadow wing up and then a big spear thrust out followed by an eye and head and dorsal fin and the tuna jumps with the wave and he's missed it.

"Marlin," Carlos yells from the top of the house and stamps his feet up and down, the signal that a fish is raised. He swarms down to the wheel and you go back to where the rod rests in its socket and there comes the shadow again, fast as the shadow of a plane moving over the water, and the spear, head, fin and shoulders smash out of water and you hear the click the closepin makes as the line pulls out and the long bight of line whishes through the water as the fish turns and as you hold the rod, you feel it double and the butt kicks you in the belly as you come back hard and feel his weight, as you strike him again and again, and again.

Then the heavy rod arc-ing out toward the fish, and the reel in a band-saw zinging scream, the marlin leaps clear and long, silver in the sun long, round as a hogshead and banded with lavender stripes and, when he goes into the water, it throws a column of spray like a shell lighting.

Then he comes out again, and the spray roars, and again, then the line feels slack and out he bursts headed across and in, then jumps wildly twice more seeming to hang high and stiff in the air before falling to throw the column of water and you can see the hook in the corner of his jaw.

Then in a series of jumps like a greyhound he heads to the northwest and standing up, you follow him in the boat, the line taut as a banjo string and little drops coming from it until you finally get the belly of it clear of that friction against the water and have a straight pull out toward the fish.

And all the time Carlos is shouting, "Oh, God the bread of my children! Oh look at the bread of my children! Joseph and Mary look at the bread of my children jump! There it goes the bread of my children! He'll never stop the bread the bread the bread of my children!"

This striped marlin jumped, in a straight line to the northwest, fifty-three times, and every time he went out it was a sight to make your heart stand still. Then he sounded and I said to Carlos, "Get me the harness. Now I've got to pull him up the bread of your children."

"I couldn't stand to see it," he says. "Like a filled pocket-book jumping. He can't go down deep now. He's caught too much air jumping."

"Like a race horse over obstacles," Julio says. "Is the harness all right? Do you want water?"

"No." Then kidding Carlos, "What's this about the bread of your children?"

"He always says that," says Julio. "You should hear him curse me when we would lose one in the skiff."

"What will the bread of your children weigh?" I ask with mouth dry, the harness taut across shoulders, the rod a flexible prolongation of the sinew pulling ache of arms, the sweat salty in my eyes.

"Four hundred and fifty," says Carlos.

"Never," says Julio.

"Thou and thy never," says Carlos. "The fish of another always weighs nothing to thee."

"Three seventy-five," Julio raises his estimate. "Not a pound more."

Carlos says something unprintable and Julio comes up to four hundred.

The fish is nearly whipped now and the dead ache is out of raising him, and then, while lifting, I feel something slip. It holds for an instant and then the line is slack.

"He's gone," I say and unbuckle the harness.

"The bread of your children," Julio says to Carlos.

"Yes," Carlos says. "Yes. Joke and no joke yes. *El pan*

de mis hijos. Three hundred and fifty pounds at ten cents a pound. How many days does a man work for that in the winter? How cold is it at three o'clock in the morning on all those days? And the fog and the rain in a norther. Every time he jumps the hook cutting the hole a little bigger in his jaw. Ay how he could jump. How he could jump!"

"The bread of your children," says Julio.

"Don't talk about that any more," said Carlos.

No it is not elephant hunting. But we get a kick out of it. When you have a family and children, your family, or my family, or the family of Carlos, you do not have to look for danger. There is always plenty of danger when you have a family.

And after a while the danger of others is the only danger and there is no end to it nor any pleasure in it nor does it help to think about it.

But there is great pleasure in being on the sea, in the unknown wild suddenness of a great fish; in his life and death which he lives for you in an hour while your strength is harnessed to his; and there is satisfaction in conquering this thing which rules the sea it lives in.

Then in the morning of the day after you have caught a good fish, when the man who carried him to the market in a handcart brings the long roll of heavy silver dollars wrapped in a newspaper on board it is very satisfactory money. It really feels like money.

"There's the bread of your children," you say to Carlos.

"In the time of the dance of the millions," he says, "a fish like that was worth two hundred dollars. Now it is thirty. On the other hand a fisherman never starves. The sea is very rich."

"And the fisherman always poor."

"No. Look at you. You are rich."

"Like hell," you say. "And the longer I fish the poorer I'll be. I'll end up fishing with you for the market in a dinghy."

"That I never believe," says Carlos devoutly. "But look. That fishing in a dinghy is very interesting. You would like it."

"I'll look forward to it," you say.

"What we need for prosperity is a war," Carlos says. "In the time of the war with Spain and in the last war the fishermen were actually rich."

"All right," you say. "If we have a war you get the dinghy ready."

Appendix II

Two-page autograph letter is accompanied by an envelope signed in pencil, addressed in Hemingway's hand to "Erl Roman Esq. / Miami Herald / Miami / Fla." And signed by Hemingway on the verso, "E. Hemingway / Yacht Pilar / Bimini / B.W.I."

Will make this very short on acct. Bill Fagen leaving. May 8 [1935]

Dear Erl,
    Yesterday May 7 Henry H. STRATER, widely known painter, of OGUNQUIT Maine, Pres. Maine Tuna Club, fishing with me on Pilar landed Blue Marlin which weighed 500 lbs. on tested scales after all of meat below anal fin had been torn away by sharks when fish was brought to gaff – Had him ready to take in when sharks hit him – Fish 12 feet 8½ inches – Tail 48 inch spread – girth 62 in. (will send

~~all other exact measurements when have chance to use steel tape on him)~~ Fish hooked off Bimini, hooked in corner of mouth, never layted, jumped 18 times clear, brought to boat in an hour such a heavy fish jumped hell out of himself. We worked him fast our system. Had him at boat when shark hit him. Strater has football knee, went out of joint, had hell with it, we wouldnt handline fish, he got him up himself, in one hour 40 minutes, we got him over the roller after <u>Some</u> lifting boy, all blood drained, meat gone below anal fin to tail, but fish completely intact, Fred Parke is mounting it –

Had two buckets full of meat that knocked off but wouldnt weigh it as didnt want try to beat Tommys record with any conniving.

Fish would have weighed between 700 and 900 – He weighed 500 before 20 some witnesses. We could have brought him plenty up above that by weighing the loose meat. Same day I landed 128 lb. white Marlin on light outfit and a 68 lb. white Marlin –

Straters fish on 12-0 Vom Hofe – Vom Hofe 20 oz Hickory tip – 39 thread – strip dolphin belly, 15 foot cable – 11/0 Pflueger Sobey hook –

One other boat caught fish – Bill Fagen – Fish was hit by shark same way as the record Zane Grey 1040 lb. fish was – with 5 minutes more would have had him – was reaching for leader when they hit him.

Dont know anything more this morning except I would trade you this hangover for any reasonable offer –

On board boat 1 Strater, Dr. McCullough (Bill has his initials) me, Albert Pinder, Key West, and Hamilton Adams, Key West,

Please copyright any and all Pics in my name – Take best one out of pack I'm sending for the Paper – Please Send all back by Bill Fagen on Sunday.

Have tropical camera place do 2 of each and send prints and negatives by Bill – $6.00 enclosed for expenses – Will pay Bill if costs more –

Appendix III

ERNEST HEMINGWAY'S

LIST OF PRINCIPAL SHARKS

IN CUBAN WATERS

Ernest Hemingway's list of sharks in Cuban waters. Two-page typewritten list preserved in two drafts, the first with handwritten annotations (see fig. 10). Ernest Hemingway Personal Papers, Stories and Fragments, Box MS57, Folder 10, at the John F. Kennedy Presidential Library and Museum, Boston.

Principal Sharks in Cuban Waters		
Local Name	**English Name**	**Remarks**
DENTUSO	Mako Shark	Rare. Vicious. Grows to 1000 pounds and over. Could be man-eater but ordinarily follows schools of mackerel and swordfish.

CORNUDA	Hammerhead	Common, especially in spring and summer. Frequents entrances of harbours and small rivers and along reefs. Is definitely a man-eating shark and reaches weights of 1200 and over. Rarely attacks during breeding period in April.
CABEZA BATEA	Tiger Shark	Abundant, slow, stupid shark which will eat anything from garbage to gasoline tins. When blood is present in water, will attack anything including man. Reaches 1000 pounds but most common at 400-600 pounds. They have been known to take bathers from the rocky beaches off the Punta Brava at Havana and if they have become man eaters, are dangerous.
GALANO	Shovel Nose	Most common Cuban shark and the most consistently dangerous. If hungry they will attack anything. If not hungry they are shy and wary. They are found in all parts of the Gulf Stream and will come instantly to the scent of blood. Have a fine sense of smell – will come where any objects dropped in the water especially those containing grease or anything nauseous. The smell of blood maddens them, so that they will attack blindly even when wounded.

TIBURON DE LEY	White Shark or True Shark	Comparatively rare. Have never known them to be man-eaters as they are comparatively shy and never attack hooked fish. Reach great weight. Much nonsense has been written about this shark as a man-eater. Off Cuban coast, those sharks which have attacked human beings, have been the Hammerhead, Galano, or Tiger Shark. The Mako will rush at a man who has him hooked but he is primarily a fish-eating shark and there are no instances of his ever having attacked human beings, as far as I know.
BOCA DULCE	Blue-Fin or Soup-Fin Shark	An exceedingly shy fish-eating shark which is only caught at night. No instances of ever attacking human beings.
GATA	Nurse Shark	Abundant in shallows. Has no teeth. Dark brown in colour. Absolutely inoffensive.
ZORRO	Thresher Shark	Very shy shark in deep water. Never attacks human beings, nor hooked fish.

	Black-Tip Shark or Mackerel Shark	Rarely goes over three hundred pounds. Plump, full bodied, extremely voracious. A fish shark which might, and has, attacked men who have had fish slime or fish blood on them and might attack a man who is bleeding. Runs, usually with the schools of migratory fish such as kingfish, bonito, etc.

Notes:

Believe any tests of repellant are valueless unless sharks have a live, bleeding object to stimulate their appetites. Their behaviour when there is no blood in the water is completely distinct from when there is blood. For a repellant to have any value conditions of wounded men in the water must be simulated, either by bleeding porpoise, or blackfish, bleeding fish, or a bleeding warm blooded animal such as a pig. I myself would consider any tests of a repellant valueless unless it were made under such conditions. A shark can change from a comparatively harmless object to a definite danger the instant it smells blood. Without plenty of fresh blood from a live object in the water, any repellant tests will be worthless.

E.H.

Appendix IV

"Pursuit As Happiness,"

A Previously Unpublished

Short Story

Untitled short story preserved as a twenty-two-page typescript with pencil corrections in the author's hand (see fig. 11). Ernest Hemingway Collection, Item 733, Manuscript Series, Box 59, Folder 19, at the John F. Kennedy Presidential Library and Museum, Boston.

Pursuit As Happiness

That year we had planned to fish for marlin off the Cuban coast for a month. The month started the tenth of April and by the tenth of May we had twenty five marlin and the charter was over. The thing to have done then would have been to buy some presents to take back to Key West, fill the *Anita* with just a little more than the expensive Cuban gas necessary to run across, get cleared and go home. But the big fish had not started to run.

"Do you want to try her another month, Cap?" Mr. Josie asked. He owned the *Anita* and was chartering her for ten dollars a day. The standard charter price then was thirty five a day. "If you want to stay I can cut her to nine dollars."

"Where would we get the nine dollars?"

"You pay me when you get it. You got good credit with the Standard Oil Company at Belot across the bay and when we get the bill I can pay them from last month's charter money. If we get bad weather you can write something."

"All right," I said and we fished another month. We had forty two marlin by then and still the big ones had not come. There was a dark, heavy stream close in to the Morro, sometimes there would be acres of bait, and there were flying fish going out from under the bows and birds working over the water all the time. But we had not raised one of the huge marlin although we were catching, or losing, white marlin each day and on one day I caught five.

We were very popular along the water front because we butchered all our fish and gave them away and when we would come in past the Morro Castle and up the channel toward the San Francisco docks with a marlin flag up you could see the crowd starting to run for the docks. The fish was worth from eight to twelve cents a pound that year to a fisherman and twice that in the market. The day we came in with five flags the police had to charge the crowd with clubs. It was ugly and bad. But that was an ugly and bad year ashore.

"The goddam police running off our regular clients and getting all the fish," Mr. Josie said. "To hell with you," he told a policeman that was reaching down for a ten pound piece of marlin. "I never saw your ugly face before. What's your name?"

The policeman gave his name.

"Is he in the <u>compromiso</u> book, Cap?"

"Nope."

The <u>compromiso</u> book was the book where we wrote down the names of people to whom we had promised fish.

"Write him down in the <u>compromiso</u> book for next week for a small piece, Cap," Mr. Josie said. "Now police you go the hell away from here and club somebody that isn't friends of ours. I seen enough damn police in my life. Go on. Take the club and the pistol both and get off the dock unless you're a dock police."

Finally the fish was all butchered out and apportioned according to the book and the book was full of promises for a week.

"You go on up to the Ambos Mundos and get washed up Cap and take a shower and I'll meet you there. Then we can go up to the Floridita and talk things over. That police got on my nerves."

"You come on up and take a shower too."

"No. I can clean up good on her here after Carlos cleans. I didn't sweat like you did today."

So I walked up the cobbled street that was the short cut to the Ambos Mundos Hotel and checked if I had any mail at the desk and then rode up in the elevator to the top floor. My room was on the north east corner and the trade wind blew through the windows and made it cool. I looked out of the window at the roofs of the old part of town and across at the harbour and watched the *Orizaba* go out slowly down the harbour with all her lights on. I was tired from working so many fish and I felt like going to bed. But

I knew if I lay down I might go to sleep so I sat on the bed and looked out the window and watched the bats hunting and then finally I undressed and took a shower and got into some fresh clothes and went downstairs. Mr. Josie was waiting in the doorway of the hotel.

"You must be tired, Ernest," he said.

"No," I lied.

"I'm tired," he said. "Just from watching you pull on fish. That's only two under our all time record. Seven and the eye of an eighth." Neither Mr. Josie nor I liked to think of the eye of the eighth fish but we always stated the record in this way.

We were walking up the narrow side-walk on Obispo street and Mr. Josie was looking in all the lighted windows of the shops. He never bought anything until it was time to go home. But he liked to look at everything there was for sale. We passed the last two lighted stores and the lottery ticket office and pushed open the swinging door of the old Floridita.

"You better sit down, Cap," Mr. Josie said.

"No. I feel better standing up at the bar."

"Beer," said Mr. Josie. "German beer. What you drinking, Cap?"

"Frozen Daiquiri without sugar."

Constante made the Daiquiri and left enough in the shaker for two more. I was waiting for Mr. Josie to bring up the subject. He brought it up as soon as his beer came.

"Carlos says they got to come in this next month," he said. Carlos was our Cuban mate and a great commercial marlin fisherman. "He says he never saw such a current and when they come they'll be something like we never seen. He says they've got to come."

"He told me too."

"If you want to try another month, Cap, I can make her eight dollars a day and I can cook instead of we wasting money on sandwiches. We can run into the cove for lunch and I'll cook in there. We're getting those wavy striped bonita all the time. They're as good as little tuna. Carlos says he can pick us up stuff cheap in the market when he goes for bait. Then we can eat supper nights in the Perla of San Francisco restaurant. I ate there good last night for thirty five cents."

"I didn't eat last night and saved money."

"You got to eat Cap. That's maybe why you're a little tired today."

"I know it. But are you sure you want to try another month?"

"She don't have to be hauled out for another month. Why should we leave it when the big ones are coming?"

"You have anything to do you'd rather do?"

"No. You?"

"No. Do you think they'll really come?"

"Carlos says they've got to come."

"Then suppose we hook one and we can't handle him on this tackle we have."

"We got to handle him. You can stay with him forever if you eat good. And we're going to eat good. Then I've been thinking about something else."

"What?"

"If you go to bed early and don't have any social life you can wake up at daylight and start to write and you can get a day's work done by eight o'clock. Carlos and I'll have everything ready to go and you just step on board."

"Okay," I said. "No social life."

"That social life is what wears you out, Cap. But I don't mean none at all. Just take it on Saturday nights."

"Fine," I said. "Social life on Saturday nights only. Now what would you suggest I write?"

"That's up to you, Cap. I don't want to interfere with that. You always did good when you worked."

"What would you like to read?"

"Why don't you write good short stories about Europe or Out West or when you were on the bum or war or that sort of thing. Why don't you write one about just things that you and I know? Write one about what the *Anita*'s seen. You could put in enough social life to make it appeal to everybody."

"I'm laying off social life."

"Sure, Cap. But you got plenty to remember. Laying off won't harm you now."

"No," I said. "Thank you very much Mr. Josie. I'll start working in the morning."

"What I think we ought to do before we start on the new system is for you to eat a big rare steak tonight so you'll be strong tomorrow and wake up wanting to work and fit to fish. Carlos says the big ones can come any day now. Cap you got to be at your best for them."

"Do you think one more of these would do me any harm?"

"Hell no, Cap. All they got in them is rum and a little lime juice and maraschino. That isn't going to hurt a man."

Just then two girls we knew came into the bar. They were very nice looking girls and they were fresh for the evening.

"The fishermen," one said in Spanish.

"The two big healthy fishermen in from the sea," the other girl said.

"N.S.L.," Mr. Josie said to me.

"No social life," I confirmed.

"You have secrets?" one of the girls asked. She was an awfully nice looking girl and on this profile you could not see the slight imperfection where some early friend's right hand had marred the complete purity of the line of her rather beautiful nose.

"The Cap and I are talking business," Mr. Josie said to the two girls and they went down to the far end of the bar. "You see how easy it is?" Mr. Josie asked. "I'll handle the social end and all you have to do is get up in the mornings early and write and be in shape to fish. Big fish. The kind that can run over a thousand pounds."

"Why don't we trade," I said. "I'll handle the social life and you get up early in the mornings and write and keep yourself in shape to fish big fish that can run over a thousand pounds."

"I'd be glad to, Cap," Mr. Josie said seriously. "But you're the one of us two that can write. And you're younger than me and better suited to handle the fish. I'm putting in the boat at just what I figure is probably the depreciation on the engine running her the way we do."

"I know it," I said. "I'll try and write well too."

"I want to keep proud of you," Mr. Josie said. "And I want us to catch the biggest goddam marlin that ever swam in the ocean and weigh him honest and cut him up and give him away to the poor people we know and not one piece to any damn clubbing police in the country."

"We'll do it."

Just then one of the girls waved to us from the far end of the bar. It was a slow night and there was no one but us in the place.

"N.S.L." Mr. Josie said.

"N.S.L." I repeated ritually.

"Constante," Mr. Josie said. "Ernesto here wants a waiter. We're going to order a couple of big rare steaks."

Constante smiled and raised his finger for a waiter.

As we passed the girls to go into the dining room one of the girls put out her hand and I shook it and whispered solemnly in Spanish, "N.S.L."

"My God," the other girl said. "They're in politics and in a year like this." They were impressed and a little frightened.

In the morning when the first daylight from across the bay woke me I got up and started to write on a story that I hoped Mr. Josie would like. It had the *Anita* in it and the water front and the things we knew that had happened and I tried to get into it the feeling of the sea and the things we saw and smelt and heard and felt each day. I worked on the story every morning and we fished each day and caught good fish. I trained hard and fought all the fish standing instead of sitting in a chair. And still the big fish had not come.

One day we saw one towing a commercial fisherman's dinghy with the dinghy down by the bows and the marlin makeing splashes as a speed boat would each time he jumped. That one broke off. One day, in a rain squall, we saw four men trying to hoist one, wide and deep and dark purple into a skiff. That marlin dressed out five hundred pounds and I saw the huge steaks cut from him on the marble slab in the old market.

Then, on a sunny day, with a heavy dark stream the water so clear and in so close that you could see the shoals in the mouth of the harbour ten fathoms deep we hit our first big fish just outside the Morro. In those days there were no outriggers and no rod holders and I was just letting out a light rig hopeing to pick up a kingfish in the channel when this fish hit. He came out in a surge and his bill looked like a sawed-off billiard cue. Behind it his head showed huge and wide and he looked as wide as a dinghy. Then he passed us in a rush with the line cutting parallel to the boat and the reel emptying so fast that it was hot to the touch. There were four hundred yards of fifteen thread line on the reel and half of it was gone by the time I had gotten into the bow of the *Anita*.

I got there by holding onto handholds we had built into the top of the house. We had practiced this run forward and the scramble over the forward deck to where you could brace against the stem of the boat with your feet. But we had never practiced it with a fish that passed you like a subway express when you are at a local station and with one arm holding the rod bucking and digging into the butt rest and with the other hand and both bare feet braking on the deck as the fish hauled you forward.

"Hook her up, Josie," I yelled. "He's takeing all of it."

"She's hooked up, Cap. There he goes."

By now I had one foot braced against the stem of the *Anita* and the other leg against the starboard anchor. Carlos was holding me around the waist and ahead of us the fish was jumping. He looked as big around as a big wine barrel when he jumped. He was silver in the bright sun and I could see the broad purple stripes down his sides. Each time he jumped he made a splash like a horse falling off a cliff and he jumped and jumped and jumped. The reel was too hot to hold and the core of line on it was getting thinner and thinner in spite of the *Anita* going full speed after the fish.

"Can you get any more out of her?" I called to Mr. Josie.

"Not in this world," he said. "What you got left?"

"Damn little."

"He's big," Carlos said. "He's the biggest marlin I've ever seen. If he'll only stop. If he'll only go down. Then we'll run up on him and get line."

The fish made his first run from just off the Morro Castle to opposite the Nacional Hotel. That is about the way we went. Then with less than twenty yards of line on the reel he stopped and we ran up on him recovering line all the time. I remember that there was a Grace Line ship ahead of us with the black pilot boat going out to her and I was worried that we might be on her course as she came in. Then I remember watching her while I reeled and then working my way back to the stern and watching the ship pick up her speed. She was coming in well outside of us and the pilot boat would not foul us either.

Now I was in the chair and the fish was straight up and down and we had a third of the line on the reel. Carlos had poured sea water on the reel to cool it and he poured a bucket of water over my head and shoulders.

"How are you doing, Cap?" Mr. Josie asked.

"Okay."

"You didn't hurt yourself up in the bow?"

"No."

"Did you ever think there was a fish like that?"

"No."

"Grande. Grande," Carlos kept saying. He was trembling like a bird dog; a good bird dog. "I've never seen such a fish. Never. Never. Never."

We did not see him again for an hour and twenty minutes. The current was very strong and it had carried us down to opposite Cojimar which is about six miles from where the fish first sounded. I was tired but my hands and feet were in good shape and I was getting line on him now quite steadily being careful never to pull harshly nor to jerk. I could move him now. It wasn't easy. But it was possible if you kept the line just this side of the breaking point.

"He's going to come up," Carlos said. "Sometimes the great ones do that and you can gaff them while they are still innocent."

"Why does he come up now?" I asked.

"He's puzzled," Carlos said. "And you're leading him. He doesn't know what it is about."

"Don't ever let him find out," I said.

"He'll weigh 900 dressed out," Carlos said.

"Keep your mouth off of him," Mr. Josie said. "You want to work him any different, Cap?"

"No."

When we saw him we knew how really big he was. You cannot say it was frightening. But it was awesome. We saw him slow and quiet and almost unmoving in the water with his great pectoral fins like two long purple scythe blades. Then he saw the boat and the line started to race off the reel as though we were hooked to a motor car and he started jumping out to the northwest with the water pouring from him at each jump.

I had to go into the bow again and we chased him until he sounded. This time he went down almost opposite the Morro. Then I worked my way back to the stern again.

"Do you want a drink, Cap?" Mr. Josie asked.

"No," I said. "Get him to put some oil in the reel and not spill it and put some more salt water on me."

"Can't I get you anything really, Cap?"

"Two hands and a new back," I said. "The son of a bitch is as fresh as he was at the start."

The next time we saw him was an hour and a half later well past Cojimar and he jumped and ran again and I had to go in the bow while we chased him.

When I got back to the stern and could sit down again Mr. Josie said, "How is he, Cap?"

"He's just the same as always. But the temper is starting to go out of the rod."

The rod was bent like a full drawn bow. But now when I lifted it did not straighten as it should.

"She's still got some left," Mr. Josie said. "You can stick with him forever, Cap. You want some more water on your head?"

"Not yet," I said. "I'm worried about the rod. His weight has just taken the temper out."

An hour later the fish was comeing in steadily and well and he was makeing big slow circles.

"He's tired," Carlos said. "He's going to come in easy now. The jumping has filled up his air sacs and he can't go deep."

"The rod's gone," I said. "She won't straighten at all now."

It was true. The rod's tip now touched the surface of the water and when you lifted to raise the fish and to reel to take up line the rod did not re-act. It was not a rod anymore. It was like a projection of the line. It was still possible to gain a few inches of line each time you lifted. But that was all.

The fish was moveing in slow circles and as he moved on the outgoing half of the circle he took line off of the reel. On the incoming circle you gained it back. But with the temper gone out of the rod you could not punish him and you had no command over him at all.

"It's bad, Cap," I said to Mr. Josie. "If he'd decide to go down now to die we'd never get him up."

"Carlos says he's coming up. He says he caught so much air jumping he can't go deep and die. He says this is the way the big ones always act at the end when they've jumped a lot. I counted him jump thirty six times and maybe I missed some."

This was the longest speech I had ever heard Mr. Josie make and I was impressed. Just then the big fish started down and down and down. I was braking with both hands on the drum of the reel and keeping the line almost at breaking point and feeling the metal of the reel drum revolve in slow jerks under my fingers.

"How's the time?" I asked Mr. Josie.

"You've been with him three hours and fifty minutes."

"I thought you said he couldn't go down and die," I said to Carlos.

"Hemingway he has to come up. I know he has to come up."

"Tell him so," I said.

"Get him some water, Carlos," Mr. Josie said. "Don't talk, Cap."

The ice water felt good and I spit it out onto my wrists and told Carlos to pour the rest of the glass on the back of my neck. The sweat salted the places on my shoulders where the harness had rubbed them bare but it was so hot in the sun that there was no warm feeling from the blood. It was a July day and the sun was at noon.

"Put some more salt water on his head," Mr. Josie said. "With a sponge."

Just then the fish stopped takeing out line. He hung steady for a time feeling as solid as though you were hooked to a concrete pier and then slowly he started up. I recovered the line; reeling with the wrist alone as there was no spring in the rod at all and it was limp as a weeping willow.

When the fish was about a fathom under the surface so that we could see him looking like a long purple striped canoe with two great jutting wings he started to circle slowly. I held all the tension I could on him to try and shorten the circle. I was holding up to that absolute hardness that indicates the breaking strength of the line when the rod let go. It did not break sharply or suddenly. It just collapsed.

"Cut thirty fathoms of line off the big rig," I said to Carlos. "I'll hold him on the circles and when he's coming in we can get enough line to make this line fast to the big line and I'll change rods."

There was no question any more of catching the fish as a world's record or any other sort of record since the rod was broken. But he was a whipped fish now and on the heavy gear we should get him. The only problem was that the big rod was too stiff for the fifteen thread line. That was my problem and I would have to work it out.

Carlos was stripping white thirty six thread line off the big Hardy reel measureing it with his arms extended as he pulled it out through the guides of the rod and dropped it on the deck. I held the fish all that I could with the useless rod and saw Carlos cut the white line and pull a long length of it through the guides.

"All right, Cap," I said to Mr. Josie. "You take this line now when he comes in on his circle and take in enough so Carlos can make the two lines fast. Just take it in soft and easy."

The fish came in steadily as he rounded on his circle and Mr. Josie brought the line in foot by foot and passed it to Carlos who was knotting it to the white line.

"He's got them tied," Mr. Josie said. He still had about a yard of the green fifteen thread line to spare and was holding the live line in his fingers as the fish came to the inside limit of his circle. I broke my hands loose from the small rod, laid it down, and took the big rod that Carlos handed me.

"Cut away when you are ready," I said to Carlos. To Mr. Josie I said, "Let your slack out soft and easy, Cap and I'll use a light, light drag until we get the feel of it."

I was watching the green line and the great fish when Carlos cut. Then I heard a cry such as I have never heard a sane human being make. It was as though you could distill all of despair and make it into a sound. Then I saw the green line slowly going through Mr. Josie's fingers and then watched it go on down, down and out of sight. Carlos had cut the wrong loop of the knots he had made. The fish was out of sight.

"Cap," Mr. Josie said. He did not look very well. Then he looked at his watch. "Four hours and twenty two minutes," he said.

I went down to see Carlos. He had been vomiting in the

head and I told him not to feel bad that it could happen to anyone. His brown face was all tied up and he was talking in a low strange voice so you could hardly hear him.

"All my life fishing and I never saw such a fish and I did that. I've ruined your life and my life."

"Hell," I told him. "You mustn't talk nonsense like that. We'll catch plenty of bigger fish." But we never did.

Mr. Josie and I sat in the stern and let the *Anita* drift. It was a lovely day on the Gulf with only a light breeze and we looked at the shore line with the small mountains showing behind it. Mr. Josie was putting mercurochrome on my shoulders and on my hands where they had stuck to the rod and on the soles of my bare feet where the skin was chafed through. Then he mixed two whisky sours.

"How's Carlos?" I asked.

"He's pretty broke up. He's just crouching down there."

"I told him not to blame himself."

"Sure. But he's down there blameing himself."

"How do you like the big ones now?" I asked.

"It's all I ever want to do," Mr. Josie said. "Did I handle her all right for you Cap?"

"Hell yes."

"No. Tell me true."

"I told you true."

"The charter's supposed to be up today. Now I'll fish her for nothing if you want."

"No."

"I'd rather it was that way. Do you remember him going up toward the National Hotel like nothing in the world?"

"I remember everything about him."

"Have you been writing good, Cap? It isn't too hard doing it in the early mornings?"

"I've been writing as good as I can."

"You keep it up and everybody is all right for always."

"I may lay off it tomorrow morning."

"Why?"

"My back's bad."

"Your head's all right isn't it. You don't write with your back."

"My hands will be sore."

"Hell, you can hold a pencil. You'll find in the morning you'll probably feel like it."

Strangely enough I did and the next day I worked well and we were out of the harbour at eight o'clock and it was another perfect day with just a light breeze and the current in close to the Morro Castle as it had been the day before. On that day we did not put out any light rig when we hit the clear water. We had done that once too often. I slacked out a big Cero mackerel that weighed about four pounds from the one really big outfit we had. It was the heavy Hardy rod and the reel with the white thirty six thread line and it was a good big outfit for those days. Carlos had spliced back on the twenty fathoms of line he had taken off the day before and the five inch reel was full. The only trouble was the rod was too stiff. In big game fishing a rod that is too stiff kills the angler while a rod that bends properly kills the fish.

Carlos only spoke when spoken to and he was still in his sorrow. I could not afford any sorrow because I ached too much and Mr. Josie was never much of a man for sorrow.

"All he's been doing all morning is shakeing his goddamn head," he said. "He's not going to bring any fish back that way."

"How do you feel, Cap?" I asked. We called each other Cap interchangeably.

"I feel good," Mr. Josie said. "I went up town last night and sat and listened to that all girl orchestra on the square and drank a few bottles of beer and then I went to Donovan's. There was hell in there."

"What kind of hell?"

"No good hell. Bad. Cap I'm glad you weren't along."

"Tell me about it," I said holding the rod well out to the side and high so that the big mackerel skipped at the edge of the wake. Carlos had turned the *Anita* to follow the edge of the stream along past the fortress of Cabanas. The white cylinder of the teaser was jumping and darting in the wake and Mr. Josie had settled in his chair and was slacking out another big mackerel bait on his side of the stern.

"In Donovan's there was a man claimed he was a Captain in the secret police. He said he liked my face and he said he'd kill any man in the place for me as a present. I tried to quiet him down. But he said he liked me and he wanted to kill somebody to prove it. He was one of those special Machado police. Those clubbing police."

"I know them."

"I guess you do, Cap. Anyway I'm glad you weren't there."

"What did he do?"

"He kept wanting to kill somebody to show how much he liked me and I kept telling him it wasn't necessary and to just have a drink and forget about it. So he would quiet down a little and then he would want to kill somebody again."

"He must have been a nice fellow."

"Cap he was worthless. I tried to tell him about the fish so as to take his mind off of it. But he said, 'Shit on your fish. You never had any fish. See?' So I said, 'Okay shit on the fish. Let's settle for that and you and me both go home.'

"'Go home hell,' he says. 'I'm going to kill somebody for you for a present and shit on the fish. There wasn't any fish. You got that straight?'

"So then I said good night to him, Cap and I gave my money to Donovan and this police knocks it off the bar onto the floor and puts his foot on it. 'Like hell you're going home,' he said. 'You're my friend and you're going to stay here.' So I said good night to him and I said to Donovan, 'Donovan I'm sorry your money's on the floor.' I didn't know what this police would try to do and I didn't care. I was going home. So as soon as I start for home this police hauls out his gun and starts to pistol whip a poor damn Gallego that was in there drinking a beer that never'd opened his mouth all night. Nobody did anything to the police. I didn't either. I'm ashamed, Cap."

"It isn't going to last much longer now," I said.

"I know it. Because it can't. But what I didn't like the most was that police saying he liked my face. What the hell kind of face have I got Cap that a police like that would say he liked it?"

I liked Mr. Josie's face very much too. I liked it more than almost anybody's face I know. It had taken me a long time to appreciate it because it was a face that had not been sculptured for a quick or facile success. It had been formed at sea, on the profitable side of bars, playing cards with other gamblers, and by enterprises of great risk conceived and undertaken with cold and exact intelligence. No part of the face was handsome except the eyes which were a lighter and stranger blue than the Mediterranean is on its brightest and clearest day. The eyes were wonderful and the face was certainly not beautiful and now it looked like blistered leather.

"You have a good face, Cap," I said. "Probably the only good thing about that son of a bitch was that he could see it."

"Well I'm going to stay out of joints now until this business is over," Mr. Josie said. "Sitting there on the square with the all girl orchestra and that girl that sings it was fine and wonderful. How do you really feel, Cap?"

"I feel pretty bad," I said.

"It didn't hurt you in the gut? I was worried always when you were in the bow."

"No," I said. "It's in the roots of the back."

"The hands and feet don't amount to anything and I bandaged up the harness," Mr. Josie said. "It won't chafe as bad. Did you really work okay, Cap?"

"Sure," I said. "It's a hell of a habit to get into and it's just as hard to get out."

"I know a habit is a bad thing," Mr. Josie said. "And work probably kills more people than any other habit. But with you when you do it then you don't give a damn about anything else."

I looked at the shore and we were off a lime kiln close to the beach where the water was very deep and the Gulf Stream made it almost to shore. There was a little smoke comeing up from the kiln and I could see the dust of a truck comeing along the rock road on the shore. Some birds were working over a patch of bait inshore. Then I heard Carlos shout, "Marlin! Marlin!"

We all saw him at the same time. He was very dark in the water and as I watched his bill came out of the water behind the big mackerel. It was an ugly bill, round and thick and short and the fish behind it bulked hugely under the surface.

"Let him have it," Carlos yelled. "He's got it in his mouth." Mr. Josie was reeling his bait in and I was waiting for the tension that would mean that the marlin had really taken the mackerel.

Appendix V

Selected edits written in Ernest Hemingway's hand from his typescript of *The Old Man and the Sea*. The typescript is Item 90 of the Ernest Hemingway Collection at the John F. Kennedy Presidential Library and Museum in Boston. The handwritten additions are italicized below. The page numbers refer to the typescript.

1. Page 1: In the first forty days a boy had been with him. But after forty days without a fish the boy's parents had told him that the old man was *now definitely and finally,* salao, which is the worst form of unlucky, and the boy had gone *at their orders* in another boat which caught three good fish the first week. [See fig. 12.]
2. Page 8: "That's easy. I can always borrow two dollars and a half."

"I think perhaps I can too. But I try not to borrow. First you borrow, then you beg."

"Keep warm old man," the boy said. "Remember we are in September."

3. Page 12: "The great Sisler's father was never poor and he, *the father*, was playing in the big leagues when he was my age."

4. Page 12: "Baseball I think," the boy said. "Tell me about the great John J. McGraw." *He said Jota for J.*

5. Page 20: "Each line, as thick around as a big pencil, was looped onto a green-sapped stick so that any pull or touch on the bait would make the stick dip and ~~all of the lines were connected~~ *each line had two forty fathom coils in reserve which could be made fast to the other spare coils* so that, if it were necessary, a fish could take out over three hundred fathoms of line.

6. Page 26: The tuna shone silver in the sun and after he had dropped back into the water another and another rose and then they were jumping in all directions, churning the water and leaping in ~~all directions.~~ *long jumps after the bait. They were circling it and driving it.*

7. Page 27: I picked up only a straggler *from the albacore that were feeding.*

8. Page 29: *This far out* ~~Out here,~~ he must be huge in this month, he thought.

9. Page 31: Now he was ready. *He had three forty fathom coils of line in reserve* ~~beside in~~ *now as well as the coil he was using.*

10. Page 33: He must have his mouth shut tight on the wire. I wish I could see him. *I wish I could see him only once to know what I have against me.*

11. Page 33: I can do nothing with him and he can do nothing ~~to~~ *with* me, he thought. *Not as long as he keeps this up.*

12. Page 34: I wonder how the baseball came out in the grand leagues today, he thought. *It would be wonderful to do this with a radio. Then he thought, think of it always.* [In the final publication is added here: "Think of what you are doing."] *You must do nothing stupid.*

13. Page 34: Remember, no matter how little you want to, that you must eat him in the morning. *Remember he said to himself.*

14. Page 35: When the old man had gaffed her and clubbed her, holding the ~~bill~~ *rapier bill with its sand paper edge* and clubbing her *across the top of her head* until her colour turned to a colour almost like the backing of mirrors, and then, with the boy's aid hoisted her aboard; the male fish had stayed by the side of the boat. Then, while ~~he was~~ *the old man was clearing the lines and* preparing the harpoon, the male fish jumped high into the air beside the boat to see where the female was and then went down deep, his lavender wings, that were his pectoral fins, spread *wide* and all his wide lavender stripes showing. *He was beautiful, the old man remembered and he had stayed.*

15. Page 36: My choice was to go there to find him beyond all people. *Beyond all people in the world.* Now we are joined together and have been since noon.

16. Page 37: But you haven't got the boy, he thought. You have only yourself and you had better work back to the last line now, in the dark, *or not in the dark,* and cut it away and hook up the two reserve coils.

17. Page 40: There was yellow weed on the line but the old man knew that only made an added drag and he was pleased. *It was the yellow gulf weed that had made so much phosphorescence in the night.*

    "Fish," he said. "I love you and respect you very much. But I will kill you dead before this day ends."

    Let us hope so, he thought.

18. Page 48: The clouds were building up now for the trade wind and he looked ahead and saw a flight of wild ducks etching themselves *against the sky over the water,* then blurring, then etching again and he knew no man was ever alone on the sea.

19. Page 49: If there is a hurricane you always see the signs of it in the sky for days ahead if you are at sea. They do not see it ashore because they do not know what to look for, he thought. The land must make a difference too *in the shape of the clouds.* But we have no hurricane coming now.

20. Page 53: "If the fish decides to stay another night I will need to eat again and the water is low *in the bottle.*"

21. Page 55: The sun and his steady movement of his fingers had uncramped his left hand *now completely* and he began to shift more of the strain to it and he shrugged the muscles of his back to shift the hurt of the cord a little.

22. Page 57: Blood came out from under the finger nails of both ~~their~~ *his and the negro's* hands and they looked each other in the eye and at their hands and forearms and the ~~betters~~ bettors went in and out of the room and sat on high chairs against the wall and watched. *The walls were painted bright blue and were of wood and the lamps threw their shadows against them. The*

negro's shadow was huge and it moved on the wall as the breeze moved the lamps.

23. Page 64: Now go back and ~~eat~~ *prepare* the dolphin. It is too dangerous to rig the oars as a drag if you must sleep.

24. Page 65: The dolphin was cold and a *leperous* grey white now in the starlight and the old man skinned one side of him while he held his right foot on the fishes' head.

25. Page 67: He lay forward cramping himself against the line with all of his body, *putting all his weight onto his right hand,* and he was asleep.

26. Page 69: Then the line ~~came in no longer~~ *would not come in any more* and he held it until he saw the drops jumping from it in the sun. Then it started out and the old man knelt down and let it go grudgeingly back into the dark water.

    "He is makeing the far part of his circle now," he said. I must hold all I can, he thought. The strain will shorten his circle each time. Perhaps in an hour I will see him. *Now I must convince him and then I must kill him.*

27. Page 70: Just then he felt a sudden banging and jerking on the line he held with his two hands. *It was sharp and hard feeling and heavy.*

    He is hitting the wire leader with his spear, he thought. That was bound to come. *He had to do that.* It may make him jump though and I would rather he stayed circling now. ~~A few~~ *The jumps* ~~are~~ *were* necessary for him to take air. But after that each one can widen the opening of the hook wound *and he can throw the hook.*

28. Page 71: I'm tireder than I have ever been, he thought and now the trade wind is riseing. But that will be good to take him in with. *I need that badly.*

29. Page 72: But it was a fair weather breeze and he ~~would need~~ *had to have* it to get home.

30. Page 74: He felt faint again now but *he* held on the great fish all *the strain* that he could. I moved him, he thought. Maybe this time I can get him over. Pull, hands, he thought. Hold up, legs. Last for me, head. *Last for me. You never went.* This time I'll pull him over.

31. Page 75: You are killing me, fish, the old man thought. But you have a right to. Never have I seen a greater, or more beautiful, *n*or calmer or more noble thing than you, brother. Come on and kill me. *I do not care who kills who.*

32. Page 76: He took all his pain and what was left of his strength and his *long gone* pride and he put it against the fishes agony and the fish came over onto his side and swam gently on his side his bill almost touching the planking of the skiff and started to pass the boat long, *deep,* wide, silver and barred with purple and interminable in the water.

33. Page 77: Then he fell into the water with a crash that sent spray over the old man and *over* all of the skiff.
     The old man felt faint and sick *and he could not see well.*

34. Page 90: Besides, he thought. Everything kills everything else in some way. *Fishing kills me exactly as it keeps me alive. The boy keeps me alive, he thought. I must not deceive myself too much.*

35. Page 91: Then he took up the oar with the knife lashed

to it. He lifted it as lightly as he could because his hands rebelled at the pain. Then he opened and closed them on it lightly to loosen *them. He closed them firmly so they would take the pain now and ~~so they~~* would not flinch and watched the sharks come. He could see their wide, flattened, shovel-pointed heads now and their white tipped wide pectoral fins. They were ~~nasty~~ *hateful* sharks, bad smelling, scavengers as well as killers, and when they were hungry they would bite at an oar or the rudder of a boat.

36. Page 92: When he saw the shark he leaned over the side and punched at him. He hit only meat and the hide was set hard and he barely got the knife in. *The blow hurt not only his hands but his shoulder too.*

37. Page 93: "No?" the old man said and he drove the blade between the vertebrae and the brain. It was an easy shot now *and he felt the cartilage sever.*

38. Page 93: The old man wiped the blade of his knife and laid down the oar. Then he found the sheet and *the sail filled and he* brought the skiff onto her course.

39. Page 96: The old man settled himself to steer. He did not even watch the big shark sinking slowly in the water *showing first life size, then small, then tiny. That always fascinated the old man. But he did not even watch it now.* [See fig. 13.]

40. Page 98: The two sharks closed together and as he saw the one nearest him open his jaws and sink them into the *silver side of the* fish he raised the club high and brought it down heavy and slamming onto the top of the shark's broad head.

41. Pages 103–104: He jerked the tiller from the rudder and beat and chopped with it; holding it in both hands

and driveing it down against ~~all evil~~ *and again*. But they were up to the bow now and driveing in ~~again and again and~~ *one after the other and together* tearing off the pieces of meat that showed glowing below the sea as they turned to come ~~again~~ *once more*. ~~until the carcass was clean.~~

42. Page 104: He felt it go in and knowing it was sharp he drove it in again. The shark let go and rolled away. *That was the last shark of the pack that came. There was nothing more for them to eat.*

 The old man could hardly breathe now and he felt a strange taste in his mouth. It was coppery and sweet and he was afraid of it for a moment. *But there was not much of it.*

 He spat into the ocean and said, "Eat that <u>Galanos</u>. And make a dream you've killed a man."

 He knew he was beaten now *finally and without remedy* and he went back to the stern and found the jagged end of the tiller would fit in the slot of the rudder well enough for him to steer.

43. Page 105: The wind is our friend anyway, he thought. Then he added, Sometimes. And the great sea with our friends and our enemies. And bed, he thought. Bed is my friend. ~~Why did I never love bed when I had her? You did, he thought. But then you loved too many beds. But beds were all the same and the sea is a greater whore than all.~~ Just bed, he thought.

44. Page 112: "What's that?" she asked a waiter and *pointed to the* long backbone of the great fish that was now just garbage waiting to go out with the tide.

Appendix VI

Ernest Hemingway's Nobel Prize acceptance speech, delivered on December 10, 1954.

Members of the Swedish Academy, Ladies and Gentlemen:
Having no facility for speech making and no command of oratory nor any domination of rhetoric I wish to thank the administrators of the generosity of Alfred Nobel for this prize.

No writer who knows the great writers who did not receive the prize can accept it other than with humility. There is no need to list these writers. Everyone here may make his own list according to his knowledge and his conscience.

It would be impossible for me to ask the ambassador of my country to read a speech in which a writer said all of the things which are in his heart. Things may not be immediately discernable in what a man writes, and in this sometimes he is fortunate; but eventually they are quite clear and by these and the degree of alchemy (ability to make magic) that he possesses he will endure or be forgotten.

Writing, at its best is a lonely life. Organizations for writers palliate the writer's loneliness but I doubt if they improve his writing. He grows in public stature as he sheds his loneliness and often his work deteriorates. For he does his work alone and if he is a good enough writer he must face eternity, or the lack of it, each day.

For a true writer each book should be a new beginning where he tries again for something that is beyond attainment. He should always try for something that has never been done or that others have tried and failed. Then sometimes, with great luck, he will succeed.

How simple the writing of literature would be if it were only necessary to write in another way what has been well written. It is because we have had such great writers in the past that a writer is driven far out past where he can go, out to where no one can help him.

I have spoken too long for a writer. A writer should write what he has to say and not speak it. Again, I thank you.

Acknowledgments

To Patrick Hemingway I express my deepest thanks for many thought-provoking discussions about this project and his resolute collaboration through what has been a difficult year. I am grateful to Michael Katakis for his vision and support. My sincere thanks to Susan Moldow, and my editors at Simon & Schuster, Nan Graham, Daniel Loedel, and especially Kara Watson, as well as their colleagues Jeff Wilson, Brian Belfiglio, and Yessenia Santos. I am especially grateful to Alan Price, director of the John F. Kennedy Presidential Library and Museum; James Roth, deputy director; Hilary Kovar Justice, Hemingway scholar in residence at the Ernest Hemingway Collection at the John F. Kennedy Presidential Library and Museum, as well as their colleagues Maryrose Grossman and Charles Borsos of the Audiovisual Archives and particularly Stacey Chandler of the Textual Archives for their unfailing professionalism and steadfast support, without whom this work could not have been accomplished. For permission to publish my grandfather's letters in the United States I am grateful to the Ernest Hemingway Foundation and to Professor Kirk Curnutt for his kind assistance. I am grateful to Robyn Fleming of the Thomas J. Watson Library at the Metropolitan Museum of Art for assisting me with interlibrary loan requests during my research for this book and Emma Sarconi, Reference Professional for Special Collections at the Princeton University Library for assistance with the Archives of Charles Scribner's Sons. I would also like to acknowledge the following individuals: Joseph and Patricia Czapski, Angela Hemingway Charles, John Fulbrook, Carol Hemingway, Valerie Hemingway, John-Michael Maas, Bruce Schwarz, Sandra Spanier, Sarah Szeliga, and my daughter, Anouk Anji Hemingway. I am particularly grateful to my amazing wife, Colette C. Hemingway, who assisted me in the reading of my grandfather's manuscript and the selection of manuscript passages for this volume and who edited a draft of my introduction. To Colette and Anouk, with whom I have shared fishing adventures, I dedicate my work on this new edition.

Seán Hemingway

Notes to the Introduction

1   Furthermore, the blue marlin is today a threatened species. We must not allow this majestic fish, believed to be the fastest in the sea, to become extinct through human negligence.

2   In Homer's great epic poems, *The Iliad* and *The Odyssey*, which take place in the second millennium BCE, the sea is repeatedly described as "unharvestable," in contrast to the bountiful land, indicating a time before commercial fishing. See Adam Nicolson, *Why Homer Matters* (New York: Henry Holt and Company, 2014), pp. 16–19. The advent of commercial fishing ensued not long afterward and was a feature of classical civilization.

3   On the fishing logs, see Mark P. Ott, *A Sea of Change: Ernest Hemingway and the Gulf Stream. A Contextual Biography* (Kent, OH: Kent State University Press, 2008). See also William Braasch Watson, "Hemingway in Bimini: An Introduction," *North Dakota Quarterly* 63, no. 3 (Summer 1996), pp. 130–44.

4   Ernest Hemingway's chapter entitled "Marlin off Cuba" in Eugene V. Connett III's *American Big Game Fishing*, published in 1935, remains a seminal work. My grandfather held the record for the largest sailfish ever caught in the Atlantic, as well as other fishing records. In the family photo shown in figure 6, the two smaller marlin were caught by my grandfather while the other two were landed by two different fishermen.

5   See Robert McCracken Peck and Patricia Tyson Stroud, *A Glorious Enterprise: The Academy of Natural Sciences of Philadelphia and the Making of American Science* (Philadelphia: University of Pennsylvania Press, 2012), pp. 310–14. During World War II, Ernest Hemingway used the cover that the *Pilar* was on a scientific expedition for the American Museum of Natural History while Hemingway and his crew were hunting German U-boats. See Terry Mort,

The Hemingway Patrols: Ernest Hemingway and His Hunt for U-boats (New York: Scribner, 2009), especially p. 176.

6   Peck and Stroud, *A Glorious Enterprise*, fig. 14.11, p. 314.

7   Ashley Oliphant, *Hemingway and Bimini: The Birth of Sport Fishing at "The End of the World"* (Sarasota, FL: Pineapple Press), p. 67.

8   See Watson, "Hemingway in Bimini," pp. 137–38. There is a photocopy of the untitled story manuscript in the Archives of Charles Scribner's Sons, part of the Special Collections of the Firestone Library at Princeton University. However, this manuscript appears to have been part of Carlos Baker's papers and was not necessarily acquired from Ernest Hemingway before his death. I am grateful to Emma Sarconi, reference professional for Special Collections at Princeton University for her assistance with this material.

9   On the white marlin record, see ibid., pp. 130–44, especially p. 134.

10   On the waste of trophy meat in Bimini in the 1930s, see Oliphant, *Hemingway and Bimini*, pp. 132–34.

11   Ernest Hemingway to Maxwell Perkins, February 7, 1939, in Carlos Baker, ed., *Ernest Hemingway: Selected Letters, 1917–1961* (New York: Scribner, 1981), p. 479.

12   See Peter Buckley, *Ernest* (New York: Dial Press, 1978), p. 348.

13   Ernest Hemingway, *Islands in the Stream* (New York: Charles Scribner's Sons, 1970).

14   On the bottom of the box that contained the original manuscript and first typescript of *The Old Man and the Sea* is written in Hemingway's hand a pencil annotation: "The Old and the Young A Novel by Ernest Hemingway (this is one of the three books of the first volume of a three volume novel The Sea, The Air and The Land)." Ernest Hemingway Personal Papers, Other Materials, Box 5, Folder 2, at the John F. Kennedy Presidential Library and Museum.

15   See Rose Marie Burwell, *Hemingway: The Postwar Years and the Posthumous Novels* (Cambridge: Cambridge University Press, 1996), pp. 51–52.

16   Michael Reynolds, *Hemingway: An Annotated Chronology* (Detroit, MI: Omnigraphics, 1991), p. 119. On Hemingway's writing practice at the Finca, see René Villarreal and Raúl Villarreal, *Hemingway's Cuban Son: Reflections on the Writer by His Longtime Majordomo* (Kent, OH: Kent State University Press, 2009), especially pp. 16–18. See also George Plimpton, "The Art of Fiction, XXI: Ernest Hemingway," *Paris Review* 5 (Spring 1958), pp. 60–89.

17   On the relationship, see Andrea di Robilant, *Autumn in Venice:*

Ernest Hemingway and His Last Muse (New York: Alfred A. Knopf, 2018), especially p. 214 and following for the period during the writing of *The Old Man and the Sea.*

18 Mary Welsh Hemingway, *How It Was* (New York: Alfred A. Knopf, 1976), p. 310.

19 There are only three small changes in the final published text not represented in my grandfather's typescript in the Hemingway Collection.

20 The comment was published in the issue of *Life* preceding the one in which *The Old Man and the Sea* appeared. Hemingway's statement is reprinted in Matthew J. Bruccoli, ed., *Hemingway and the Mechanism of Fame* (Columbia: University of South Carolina Press, 2006), p. 121.

21 William Faulkner, review of *The Old Man and the Sea* published in *Shenandoah* 2 (Autumn 1952), p. 55.

22 Ernest Hemingway to Bernard Berenson, September 13, 1952, in Baker, *Ernest Hemingway: Selected Letters*, p. 780. Berenson considered the story "a short but not small masterpiece." See p. 785, n. 1.

23 For a thorough analysis of the book with copious citations of earlier scholarship and further reading, see Bickford Sylvester, Larry Grimes, and Peter L. Hays, *Reading Hemingway's The Old Man and the Sea: Glossary and Commentary* (Kent, OH: Kent State University Press, 2018).

24 On Hemingway's principle of the iceberg and how it relates to *The Old Man and the Sea*, see Plimpton, "The Art of Fiction," p. 84.

25 Ernest Hemingway Collection, Manuscript Series, Box 55, Folder 19, page 6, at the John F. Kennedy Presidential Library and Museum, Boston.

About the Author

Ernest Hemingway did more to influence the style of English prose than any other writer of his time. Publication of *The Sun Also Rises* and *A Farewell to Arms* immediately established him as one of the greatest literary lights of the twentieth century. Hemingway was awarded the Nobel Prize in Literature in 1954. He died in 1961.

(2) and in this sometimes he is fortunate,
but eventually they are quite clear
and by these and the degree of ↑ [ability
alchemy that he possesses he will   to work
endure or be forgotten.   magic]
¶ Writing, at its best is a lovely life.
organizations for writers palliate the
writers loneliness but I doubt if they
improve his writing. He grows in
public stature as he sheds his loneliness
and often his work deteriorates. For
he does his work alone and if he is
a good enough writer he must face
eternity, or the lack of it, each
day.

       For a true writer each book
should be a new beginning where he
tries again for something that is beyond

P-2805